SEDUCING ZEB

TARNISHED SAINTS SERIES - BOOK 4

ELIZABETH ROSE

ROSESCRIBE MEDIA INC.

AUTHOR'S NOTE

The **Tarnished Saints Series** is a twelve-book series about the twelve Taylor brothers. Each book can stand alone, but so as not to ruin any surprises it is best to read them in order if possible. Still, each book can be enjoyed by itself.

I have listed the main characters of the story as well as the Taylor men and their families for a quick reference guide for you.

I now also have an original recipe page on my site where my characters tell how to make some of the dishes they eat in the story. Just click the highlighted words if you'd like to know how to make **Zeb's Bachelor Bruschetta** or **Catalina's Breakfast Skillet**.

To find out backstory on the Taylor Twelve growing up, be sure to get your copy of the FREE **Tarnished Saints' Christmas Prequel**.

Enjoy,

Elizabeth Rose

THE TAYLOR BROTHERS

(Title and book number)

Thomas – *Doubting Thomas* – **(1)**
Matthew Levi – *Luring Levi* – **(2)**
Judas – *Judging Judas* – **(3)**
James Zebedee (Twin) – *Seducing Zeb* – **(4)**
Simon – *Saving Simon* – **(5)**
James Alphaeus (Twin) – *Wrangling James* – **(6)**
Peter – *Praising Pete* – **(7)**
Philip – *Teaching Philip* – **(8)**
John – *Loving John* – **(9)**
Nathanael – *Playing Nate* – **(10)**
Andrew – *Igniting Andrew* – **(11)**
Thaddaeus – *Taming Thad* – **(12)**

CAST OF CHARACTERS FOR SEDUCING
ZEB

James Zebedee Taylor (Zeb) – Lawyer and past stripper – identical twins with James
Catalina Rose Cordovano (Cat) – Zeb's new wife and blackjack dealer in Vegas
James Alphaeus Taylor – Zeb's twin brother – a cowboy
Crazy Aunt Penelope (Aunt Cappy) – The Taylor brothers' aunt and only sibling of their deceased father
Denny Gianopoulos – Cat's boss at the Diamond Dust Casino and her ex-boyfriend
Nate Taylor – One of Zeb's younger brothers – the musician
Thomas Taylor – The eldest of the Taylor Twelve and father to six boys: **Dan, Sam, Zeke, Josh & Jake, Eli**
Angel – Thomas' wife who has her young daughter, **Gabby** from a previous marriage
Levi Taylor – Second oldest of the Taylor brothers – Mayor of Sweetwater and half-owner of the Three Billy Goats Diner
Candace – Levi's wife – **Vance & Val** are their six-year-old twins
Judas Taylor – A brother and also Sweetwater's sheriff
Delaney (Laney) – Judas' wife and owner of the Timeless Treasures Antique Shop

Judith Delaney (J.D. or Jaydee) – their 17-year-old daughter who just had a baby boy named **Matthias**

Lorenzo Rudawski – Cat's younger brother who she thought was dead

Widow Mabel Durnsby – Sweetwater's past mayor and present busybody

Charolette Burnham – J.D.'s questionable best friend

Vincent Burley – Owner of Burley's Bar and Strip Club

Thad Taylor – The youngest of the Taylor brothers

Simon Taylor – Another brother who was once in the Navy and now works on a cruise ship

CHAPTER 1

*W*hat happens in Vegas stays in Vegas . . . unless you wake up married to the girl.

James Zebedee Taylor, or Zeb as everyone called him, woke up to the vibrating buzz of his cell phone next to his ear. He ran a weary hand over his face, feeling cold metal on his left hand that wasn't there last night.

His eyes popped open and he focused on the ring, realizing it was a wedding band. The phone buzzed again and a sick feeling lodged in the pit of his stomach as he turned his head quickly to see a woman lying next to him. Her long ebony hair was fanned out around her as she lay on her stomach with her left hand resting propped up on the pillow.

"Damn," he said aloud, seeing a matching wedding band shining on her finger. He jumped out of bed only to discover he was naked. Had one of his one-night stands gotten out of control somehow? What the hell had happened?

He quickly scooped up the phone, clicking it on, all the while his eyes staying focused on the woman in his bed that he could barely remember from last night. "Hello?" he said quietly into the phone in order not to wake the girl until he could figure out what was going on.

"Morning, Brother," came his twin brother's voice over the receiver. "Sleep well?"

"James, I really can't talk right now." Zeb turned his back to the woman and stared at the wall of the hotel room as he spoke in a low voice to his twin. James Alphaeus Taylor looked exactly like Zeb, but was much more reserved, never having done half the crazy things Zeb did in his life. Zeb put himself through law school by stripping on the weekends.

They may share the same looks and the same first name, but that was the extent of it. Their personalities were quite the opposite. Zeb was a wild bachelor who loved partying with as many women as possible, and James was more of a homebody. That is, James was a polite, respectable and somewhat shy cowboy who barely spoke to a woman unless she came up and talked to him first.

"I was calling for two reasons," continued James, not caring that Zeb wasn't in the mood for pleasantries so early in the morning. "First, since it was our birthday yesterday and I didn't arrive in Vegas until this morning, I thought we could celebrate with a brew and a rack of ribs later and maybe try our luck in the casinos."

Thirty-four years of carefree living had never ended so badly for Zeb as now. "I already celebrated last night with some of the ladies while I was waiting for you to haul your sorry ass over here from Texas," he told his brother.

"I'm sure you did," said James. "Sorry, but the closing on my ranch took longer than I'd anticipated. Things got complicated since Denise showed up insisting half my belongings were hers. I knew she'd be trouble since the day we split up."

"Well, you're just lucky you never married the girl or you'd have more to worry about than just a few missing pots and pans." He looked down at the ring on his finger, still not believing he was really married. Not after he'd been so careful to stay single for the last thirty-four years of his life. The worst part was, he couldn't remember doing it at all. Now, all his troubles began.

"If I'd married Denise in the first place instead of just living with her for the last three years like you suggested, she probably would never have left me," James reminded him. "Anyway, it sounds like you had a good time last night even without me there. Knowing you, you probably got drunk and started stripping again just to impress the ladies. So, tell me. Did you get lucky?" he asked with a chuckle on the other end of the phone.

The woman on the bed moaned slightly in her sleep and Zeb turned back to look at her. Full, lush lips, high cheekbones, and a long, straight nose were all he could see. Her eyes were closed and hidden beneath her long, dark hair. She flipped over suddenly on the bed and when she did, the sheer slip that covered her body shifted, exposing half a naked breast.

"Lucky?" he repeated his brother's words, fingering the ring with his thumb as he spoke. "Apparently so. Maybe a little luckier than I'd hoped for."

"Good for you, you silver-tongued devil. You seem to have all the luck with women. I must have missed out on that gene. Oh, that reminds me. Did you impersonate me and go on that date I set up with Ebony the blackjack dealer from the Diamond Dust Casino? After all, she's the hottest girl I've ever met. I tried to bed her the last two times I've been to Vegas. I'm pretty serious about her. I didn't want to risk the chance she'd find someone else when I didn't show, so I figured we'd pull the ol' switcheroo like we always used to do growing up."

"Oh, I don't think you have to worry about standing her up on any more dates, James."

"Why? What did she say? You know, she told me last time I was in Vegas that she wants to marry and settle down. She also said she wouldn't go to bed with a guy unless she was married to him. She told me I'm the kind of guy she's been looking for her entire life. And get this – she asked me to marry her. So I told her I'd marry her the next time I came to town. I'm not sure if she believed me, but I was serious about it. I even picked up a couple of wedding rings for the ceremony. Won't she be surprised?"

"Oh, she'll be more surprised than you think." Zeb's head pounded and he couldn't believe what his brother was telling him. He reached up and felt an egg-sized lump on his head and vaguely remembered someone hitting him last night. "James, you can't be serious. What are you trying to say? You planned on marrying a girl you just met? What the hell is the matter with you?"

"Ok – true, I don't know her well. But since she seemed so hell-bent on marrying me for some reason, I figured I'd do something crazy and impetuous. After all, you're always saying I'm boring and predictable. So, I thought I'd do something shocking. You know – I thought I'd act more like you."

"That's nothing like me," snapped Zeb. "You know I like to bed the ladies, not tie a ball and chain around my ankle. I don't even like to say the M word. My plan was always to be a bachelor my entire life."

"And you probably will be, Brother."

"Don't count on that," Zeb mumbled under his breath, glancing back to the girl on the bed.

"Zeb, I'm tired of being a bachelor and I want to settle down. Since Ebony wants to get married so badly, I figured this would be a perfect opportunity."

"Not as perfect as you think."

"Come on, Zeb, lighten up. After all, I told you I'm moving back home to Sweetwater. I decided Texas is too far away from all my brothers. With Denise gone, there's no reason for me to stay there. I decided I'd surprise Ebony by selling the ranch and bringing her back home to Michigan. I only wish I'd moved back home while Ma and Pa were still alive. But that's part of the reason I sold the ranch . . . I want the lake house and lot on

Thunder Lake that was promised to me in Pa's will. You know what I'm talking about, right? That is, the will where we have to be married to get our inheritance."

"I know exactly what you're talking about," growled Zeb. "The inheritance that I don't give a rat's ass about since I've got more money than all my brothers put together."

"Well, I care about it, so I hope you didn't ruin my chances for my inheritance by doing something stupid and chasing away Ebony."

"Well, yes and no," he said, touching the bump on his head gingerly, feeling the leftover sting.

"What are you talking about, Zeb? Did you did pose as me or not?"

"Oh, yeah. I pretended to be you all right, even if I don't know why I agreed to the lame idea in the first place."

"Zeb, calm down. We changed places in high school all the time when I needed you to pass my calculus exam or talk to a cheerleader and get a date for me. We're good at this game. Do you think Ebony believed you were me?"

Zeb held up his hand, inspecting the ring on his finger again and shook his head. "I guarantee she thought I was you."

"Hey, Zeb, sorry if I put you on the spot when I called you last night and asked you to do this for me. I know it was late and all, and I really appreciate you helping me out. This is my big chance to change my life. It's my chance to find true happiness with a beautiful woman. Even if it doesn't work out, I'll just stay married for a year so I can keep my inheritance the way Pa set up the will. After that, we'll both go our own ways."

"Oh yeah, that sounds just like true love, you idiot. You know you're just rebounding from splitting up with Denise. Besides, your plan may need a little revising," Zeb grumbled.

"Well, I just hope you two didn't get too comfortable. After all, I know the ability you have to seduce a woman – even someone like Ebony, whose legs are crossed so tight that it would take a crowbar to pry them apart. I wouldn't want you stealing her away from me now that I've managed to land a woman sexier than any you've ever had."

"Dammit, James, you are so naïve. I'm sure Ebony's not even her real name. She's a Vegas girl. She's a player. And if a girl wants to marry you before she's even checked out your goods, then she's obviously not in it for the long run. I'm sure she only wants to marry you because you've got something she wants. Once she's got her hands on it, she'll dump you just like Denise did. For God's sake, how could you let yourself be fooled by the likes of her?"

"Denise didn't dump me. It was a mutual agreement – well, sort of. Anyway, that doesn't matter. Maybe you're right, Zeb, but I don't really care. I'm not getting any younger and I want to settle down and raise a family. I've got a good feeling about this one, so I want to give her a chance. Ebony's a real looker, you have to admit."

"Oh, she's a looker all right, but just don't put too much stock in that good feeling." He glanced over to the girl sprawled out on the bed. She had kicked off the covers and her slip rode up the back of her legs, displaying a perfectly rounded derriere sporting a thong. It called to him from the bed and his groin tightened. "James, you never were a good judge of women, just admit it."

"This time will be different, you'll see. You know I still value your opinion about women, Zeb. So tell me. What do you think I should do? If you really think she's no good, then do you think I should just have you dump her for me before it's too late? Or tell her I found someone else?"

"You never could make a decision either," Zeb told him. "Sorry, James, but I'm not going to be able to do what you're suggesting. She's not the one for you, so just try to put her out of your head."

"Hey, I'm not going to be able to make something up and lie to her myself if that's what you're thinking. You know I've never been good at lying to a woman, but you're great at it. You are the one who wrote the book on that one. After all, you're a lawyer. Lying is your profession."

"I wish you would have told me all these wonderful plans yesterday. It's not going to be so easy to do what you're suggesting now."

"Why not?"

Zeb heard the bedcovers rustle and looked over his shoulder to peruse the most gorgeous woman he'd ever seen in his life sitting up and rubbing her eyes. Her long hair covered her face and, with one hand, she brushed it back behind her ear.

"I gotta go," said Zeb. "I'll catch you later."

"Wait – I'm –"

Zeb clicked off the phone with James still talking, and turned to look at his new bride. She smiled at him and then her eyes opened wide as they settled below his waist. The sight of her sexy body had gotten him fully aroused. He grabbed the cowboy hat on the bedside table he'd worn to impersonate his rancher brother and held it in front of him to hide his strong desire for her.

"James?" she said with a laugh. "What are you doing?"

"Nothing," he said, trying to sound nonchalant.

"You're playing shy again, like when I first met you, aren't you?"

"Me? Shy?"

"Well, after last night, not only me but everyone in the nightclub knows you're not the shy little cowboy you pretend to be."

"What does that mean?"

"It means you can't act coy one minute and the next be pulling off your clothes, grinding your hips against the stripper pole along with the dancers. If you think for one moment I'm going to buy the reserved act anymore, you're mistaken." She smiled her sexy smile with those lush lips and drank him in with her bedroom eyes. "Although, I have to say the whole role-reversal thing kind of excited me."

"I stripped again, did I?"

"Don't you remember?"

"I must have had too much to drink because I don't remember anything about last night. And what the hell is this?"

She was laughing until he held up his hand to show her the ring. Her big mocha brown eyes opened wide and a look of disappointment washed over her face.

"We got married," she said, looking at him cautiously from the corners of her eyes. At the same time, she sounded disgusted that he couldn't remember. "Just like we agreed upon the last time you were at my blackjack table. Why are you acting like you're changing your mind?"

"Believe me, sweetie, marriage is the last thing I'd ever want to do to myself."

"Why the sudden change of heart?" she asked. Before he could respond, she continued. "Never mind, it doesn't matter. It's too late. We're married and you can't change your mind. The deed is done and we're going to be a family now and have lots of babies and live on your ranch. You're going to teach our kids to be cowboys just like you. Or at least that's what you said."

"Really? And what are you going to teach the kids? How to bat their eyes and sway their hips to get whatever they need by luring a man in? Look, I don't know what kind of game you're playing, but I don't like the fact I've been the brunt of this cocka-mamie joke. I only wish I could remember how this all happened and how I got this lump on my head." He rubbed his fingers over his head, feeling it starting to throb more than what lay below his waist.

"I gave you that lump when you tried to mount me in the elevator on the way up here last night."

"That's right," he said, starting to remember that he was so horny last night he wanted to bang her on the way up to their room somewhere between the 10th and 12th floors. "That's not the proper way for a wife to respond to her husband on their honeymoon."

"Neither is it the way for a new husband to treat his wife. Besides, it's not a honeymoon," she told him. "If you can't control your hands in public, then you may never bed me."

"So you mean . . . we haven't consummated the wedding yet?"

She stared at him for a moment with her chin raised in the air. "No." Then she slid off the side of the bed and put her bare feet on the floor. "Not yet."

"Good," he spat. "Then we're not really married. It should be easy to get an annulment really quick." He tried to pull off the wedding ring, but it was snug and wouldn't budge from his finger. "We'll do it as soon as possible and just keep all this nonsense to ourselves, all right?"

"No!" She jumped up and put her hands on her hips. "We have to stay married, and we have to leave for your ranch in Texas right away."

He looked at her oddly, his lawyer instincts kicking in that this woman seemed panicked and also desperate to be married. There was something she wasn't telling him. He bet she had more secrets than he had right now. Before he could ask her about it, there was a knock at the door. Zeb reached down and grabbed his pants from the floor and pulled them on quickly, not bothering with underwear. It wasn't easy in his condition, but he managed to zip up his pants before he headed over to the door and pulled it open.

"Zeb, how are you feeling this morning, Sweetcakes?" The elderly woman at his door reached out and pinched him on the cheek.

"Aunt Cappy?" he asked, seeing his crazy Aunt Penelope standing there in the hallway. Everything started coming back to him now. He'd met his aunt in the casino last night and she told him she was passing through on one of her crazy trips around the United States.

"Move aside and let me in to congratulate the bride," she said, pushing her way past him into the room rather than waiting to be invited in. Aunt Penelope was his late father's sister and only sibling. She had bright red hair dyed from a bottle and wore too much makeup and ridiculously long, fake eyelashes. She was a busty woman and not much over five foot four. Her wardrobe consisted of clothes that one would expect to see only on the stages of Vegas.

"So, do you remember what happened last night?" he asked his aunt.

She turned around and narrowed her eyes as she spoke, trying to focus without having to pull out her bifocals. She always thought her glasses made her look like an old lady and would rather stumble around blindly than put them on.

"Of course I remember, you goon. I'm not senile no matter what you and your vagabond brothers think."

"That's not what I meant," he apologized and held out his hand, showing her the ring. "What I mean is . . . do you remember exactly how this happened? How I ended up getting married?"

"Why wouldn't I?" she asked. "Who do you think took you two to get married in the first place? After all, neither of you were in any shape to get behind the wheel of a car after you tasted my latest batch of mountain dew."

Zeb groaned, now realizing exactly what was in the drinks his aunt had been bringing him last night. "If I would have known it was your two hundred proof moonshine that you were slipping into my drinks I wouldn't have even touched them," he said in his defense. He'd never gotten so drunk before that he couldn't remember what he'd done. "That stuff is vile. You really need to give up making that witch's brew already."

"I didn't make it." She put her hands on her hips when she

spoke. "I told you I have a friend right here in Vegas that pulls out the bottle to celebrate every time I visit. You're just lucky I remembered how to drive after so long and was able to find that little drive-thru chapel in the dark without my glasses."

"A drive-thru chapel?" he spat, shaking his head and licking his lips, sampling the aftertaste of her friend's concoction still assaulting his taste buds. He knew they were lucky to be alive if Aunt Cappy was driving again. The whole reason she'd stopped driving years ago was because she had a habit of banging into things. It was getting too expensive hiring lawyers to get her out of the messes she'd gotten herself into since Zeb didn't want to represent her.

"Zeb, I asked you if you wanted me to take you to a drive-thru, and you agreed," said his aunt, crossing her arms over her bosom.

"Crap, Aunt Cappy, when you asked if I wanted to go to a drive-thru I thought you meant for a burger and maybe a side of greasy fries, nothing more."

"Excuse me. Why did she just call you Zeb?" came the girl's voice from the side of the bed. She pulled her dress on as she spoke.

"Because that's his name," came another voice from the hall. Zeb looked up to see James in the doorway with a look of murder in his eyes.

"James, what is this all about?" the girl asked, looking directly at Zeb.

"I'm James, he's Zeb." Zeb's twin brother stood crossing his arms over his chest, blocking the doorway entirely with his body, prohibiting any kind of mad dash out the door on Zeb's part. He greeted his aunt with a polite nod and a quick hello and then brought his attention back to the matter at hand.

Zeb felt not only a ball and chain around his ankle but the weight of the world on his shoulders right now. His head throbbed. This whole thing had turned into a big mess and, right

ELIZABETH ROSE

about now, he felt as if he hadn't a friend in the world. There was no way he was getting out of this one, no matter how cutthroat of a lawyer he was. Because now he was married to a girl he didn't know, and also to the woman of his brother's lame dreams.

"Happy Birthday," he said to himself under his breath, knowing this was going to be one birthday that neither he nor his brother would ever forget.

CHAPTER 2

$\mathcal{C}$atalina Rose Cordovano's jaw dropped, not believing that she was looking at identical twins.

"What's going on?" she asked, feeling as if her whole world just came crashing down around her.

"I'll tell you what's going on," snapped the real James, barging into the room and giving Zeb a shove. "My no-good brother was supposed to pretend to be me, but he apparently liked it more than he should have. Damn it, Zeb, you screwed me for the last time and I'm not going to let you get away with this."

"You asked him to pretend he was you?" asked Catalina, not understanding any of this.

"Just until I got here, ma'am," said James, taking off his cowboy hat and holding it against his chest and nodding politely to her.

"How dare you think you could play me like this," she spat, hating both of them right now.

"And you weren't playing him?" asked Zeb. "After all, you seemed to be in an awfully big hurry to marry a man you didn't even know and haven't had any kind of intimate relationship with. So what's your deal, Ebony? While you're at it, you might as

13

well tell us your real name instead of that stripper name you choose to hide behind."

"What makes you so sure I'm not Ebony?"

"Because I'm a lawyer, sweetie, and I've seen this before. I can tell when someone's lying."

"You're a lawyer? Not a rancher?" Her heart about beat from her chest at this announcement. She hated lawyers. Her father was a lawyer who deserted her and her mother, letting them fend for themselves as he took her brother away forever. She couldn't be married to a lawyer! This was a nightmare. She thought she was getting away from deceiving, backstabbing liars who only cared about themselves, and now she realized she had made the same mistake as her poor, departed mother.

"I'm the rancher," shouted James, thumping his thumb against his chest. "Not him."

"Not any more, you're not," Zeb reminded him, scratching the back of his neck and looking over at the far wall.

"What does that mean?" she asked.

"Are you going to tell her you sold your ranch or am I?" Zeb grinned a crazy half-smile. She felt like hitting him over the head with her shoe again like she had last night when he'd basically tried to maul her.

"Well, she knows now, you idiot," grumbled James. "Ebony, I wanted to surprise you and sell the ranch and take you back to my family in Sweetwater, Michigan. I figured it would be a great place to raise a family. I even bought us some nice rings."

"You did?" She almost choked on the words. He seemed so loving and caring, and so damned polite. He had all the qualities she'd longed for in a man her entire life. That's one of the reasons she'd asked him to marry her in the first place. Oh, why couldn't she have married him instead of his asinine, pompous, lawyer brother?

"What's the matter, sweetheart? Get caught in your own little manipulative, flirtatious game, and now you're scared you'll have to pay the price?" asked Zeb.

"The matter is that you two have played me," she retorted. "I had no idea who I was really marrying or I never would have gone through with it. How could you do such a thing?"

"Where's the marriage license?" asked Zeb, and Catalina knew she was about to be busted.

"What marriage license?" she asked, stalling for time, wondering if she'd put it in her purse, because she really couldn't remember.

"You know," said Zeb. "That little piece of paper with both our real names on it and signed by the drive-thru minister. By the way, how did you get the license issued without me being present in the first place?"

"Oh, I can answer that," said the crazy old woman Zeb had called Aunt Cappy. She stepped forward with her head down, digging through her purse that looked more like Mary Poppins' carpetbag than a handbag. The purse was huge and made from some kind of woven material that looked to her like a rug. "I took your driver's license from your wallet when you took your pants off to strip last night, Zeb. Catalina asked me to."

"Catalina?" both the boys said together.

Cat closed her eyes and shook her head. She trusted the old woman to do her dirty work, but now she'd been exposed at the wrong moment. She had hoped that information wouldn't come out until later – not in the middle of this mess right now.

The woman hadn't told her that she was the boys' aunt last night or Cat would have found another lackey to bring their drivers licenses to the County Clerk and obtain the papers to get married. She knew Bill at the County Clerk's Office right next door to the casino, and she'd slipped the old woman a twenty for her trouble. She'd sent a twenty for Bill as well so she could get the marriage license fast and with no questions asked.

"Catalina is the name on her driver's license and that's what the marriage license says, too. Oh, here it is," Cappy said, digging out a crumpled piece of paper and pulling it from the depths of her purse.

"Let me see that." James walked over and snatched it from his aunt's hand. He studied it and then glared at Cat. "You really did lie to me about your name, just like Zeb said."

"Just like I said," repeated Zeb. "If a woman wants to marry you without seeing your family jewels first, than she's not in it for the long run." Zeb pulled the paper out of his brother's hand and glanced down at it. Then he looked up at Cat. "If you'd taken the time to know who the hell you were marrying in the first place, sweetheart, you'd have seen I wasn't who you thought I was." He pushed the paper in front of her nose and she snatched it from his hand.

Glancing down at the marriage license, she read the name aloud. "James Zebedee Taylor." Then she looked up to both the boys. "How would I have known you fools were both named James? Who does something like that? What kind of crazy parents do you have, anyway?"

"We're sons of a preacher who named his twelve boys after the twelve apostles," said Zeb with a smile. "If you spent any time looking at the Bible instead of dealing cards, you'd know there were two Jameses."

"That's right," Cappy piped in. "My brother, bless his poor departed soul, had his hands full with these boys. Zeb here, for instance, knows all about the Bible because he spends more time in hotel rooms bedding girls than any of his brothers."

"Huh?" Zeb's smile turned to a frown at that announcement. It only made Catalina smile in return.

"You really did make a fool out of me, Catalina Rose Cordovano," said James, pulling a small box out of his pocket and opening it. He held up two gold, diamond-embedded wedding rings. "I thought you really wanted to marry me."

"Oh, those rings are gorgeous!" She reached out for them, but when Zeb cleared his throat, she let her hand fall to her side. She now felt very bad about what she had done.

"Those are some fine rings my brother bought for your wedding," Zeb told her. "And nothing like these that you probably got out of a box of Cracker Jack." Zeb held up his hand to prove a point, showing the plain gold band around his finger. "So why'd you do it, Catalina? Just to hustle my brother out of everything he owns?"

"It's Cat," she corrected him, telling him what she preferred to be called. "And no, it's nothing like that." She felt her throat tightening as if both the men were strangling her with just their eyes. "Don't make me sound like the only one who was deceiving anyone around here. After all, James told me he only wanted to get married to get some kind of inheritance. He said we only had to be married a year and then we could split up if we wanted to."

"Why the hell would you agree to something like that?" asked Zeb, knowing she was hiding more than she was letting on.

"Maybe I just wanted to get away from this hellhole and start a new life," she told him.

"Oh, like living a new, cozy life on a ranch that was far from here and in the middle of nowhere? Are you running from someone, Ms. Cordovano?" asked Zeb, drilling her like she was on a witness stand. "That's why you wanted someone to marry you and take you far away from here, isn't it? And that's why you were calling yourself Ebony, wasn't it? You are hiding from someone, although it's beyond me why you'd work in one of the busiest places in the world if you didn't want to be noticed."

"You're wrong!" she shouted. "I only used the name Ebony to deter all the guys in the casino always hitting on me."

"That's right, you are wrong, Zeb," said their aunt.

"Thank you." Cat acknowledged Aunt Cappy with a nod, thinking the women in the room were going to stick together, until she heard the crazy old woman's next words.

"You shouldn't call her Ms. Cordovano, Zeb," Cappy continued. "After all, she is your wife now and her proper name is Catalina Taylor. That has a nice ring to it." She took the marriage license out of Cat's hand. "I think I'll take this down to the courthouse and have it filed right away. James, be a darling and give me a ride, will you? I'm still a little shaken from having to drive these two drunkards around all night."

"It was your moonshine that got us in that condition in the first place, Aunt Cappy, so don't go making us out to look like we can't hold our liquor," said Zeb. "Now, you're not going to take that marriage license anywhere. I'm going to take care of it. We're getting an annulment as soon as possible. Here, give it to me." He held out his hand to his aunt.

"No," said James, adamantly. "You're not going to pull your strings and escape from this mess that easily. If you want out of your marriage, then do it like everyone else and without paying someone off. Come on, Aunt Cappy, I'm taking you to the courthouse and this is going to be filed. See you later, Mr. and Mrs. Taylor." He put his arm around his aunt and guided her quickly out the door.

"Well? Aren't you going to do something?" Cat asked frantically as the door closed with a thud.

"Yeah, I'm going back to bed," said Zeb, rubbing his sore head. He stripped off his pants and made himself comfortable in a lounging position. "Might as well make the best of it until the annulment goes through. Now come here, Wife," he said, patting the bed beside him.

"What for?" she asked, glaring at him out of the corner of her eye.

"Because, I believe there is the little issue of consummating the wedding that we have to address. Now, take off your clothes and scurry on over here and I'll give you a little taste of what you're going to be missing out on once we're no longer married."

Cat stood there in shock as she watched him lying on the bed with his six-pack abs and bedroom eyes. Her eyes dropped down to his nether regions and she gasped when she saw the biggest hard-on she'd ever seen on a man in her life. He chuckled and grinned like the Cheshire cat, causing her to feel a strong desire to touch him and press her body up against his.

"No!" she said. Part of her wanted to stay, but she had to go. He enticed her and disgusted her at the same time. This confused her more than she'd ever felt in her life. "Zeb Taylor, you are the biggest jerk to ever walk the earth," she said, snatching her purse from the bedside table and shoving her feet into her six-inch heeled shoes. She headed toward the door and pulled it open, only stopping briefly when she heard his response from behind her.

"That's right, Catalina Rose Taylor. I might be the biggest jerk to ever walk the earth, but you are the biggest liar. And whether you like it or not, until the annulment goes through, I'm all yours." He spread his arms out to the sides as if giving himself up as some kind of offering.

She looked back over her shoulder and he had the audacity to wink. She felt the heat flushing her face and also a tingling sensation in her groin area that was obviously only responding this way because he was lying there naked and she hadn't had sex in so long that eating a banana got her excited lately.

She thought about going back and taking him up on his offer, but she couldn't. She didn't want to ever let herself be played by a man again. She just wanted stability and security in her life and was willing to do almost anything to get it. But this wasn't the man she wanted to be married to. He was a lawyer for God's sake! He was a liar, a manipulator, and a cheat.

Just like her, she realized sadly, stepping from the room and closing the door behind her.

CHAPTER 3

"I fold," said Zeb, sliding his cards across the poker table. His brother, James, sat next to him at the little second-rate casino on the edge of Vegas called the Diamond Dust. It was small and run-down and not very crowded since it was still early in the day. Zeb would have liked to have gone to one of the classier casinos that were on the strip, but James insisted on coming here because this is where Catalina worked.

Zeb had filled out the papers for the annulment earlier, and he and Cat had signed them. Then he'd been trying to make amends with his brother the rest of the morning, but James was still sulking about the whole wedding incident. Lunch together hadn't gone well, and he only had Aunt Cappy to thank that she'd decided to invite herself and join them. It filled the awkward silence between him and James with her constant nonsensical chattering.

"Bet," mumbled James, not looking at Zeb but instead looking at his hand of cards as he pushed a few of his chips forward. He didn't have many left at all, though Zeb had quite a few.

"Call," said another player as the process continued around the table.

"You can't keep ignoring me," said Zeb, looking at the flop – the three cards faced up at the center of the table, and wondering what cards James had in his hand to actually want to place a bet.

"I can and I will," James grunted as the dealer laid down the turn card, which was a two of hearts.

"Check," James said, tapping his cards on the table, passing the betting to the next person. Zeb wasn't paying much attention to the game since he was trying his hardest to make things right between him and his brother again.

"You are being a big baby about the whole incident," said Zeb. "You're acting like I married Cat on purpose, but you know I didn't."

"Do I?" This was the first time James looked over to Zeb. The expression on his face was not pleasant.

Before Zeb knew it, the dealer laid down the river, or last card of the spread, and it was another two. When the bets were placed and came back to James, Zeb realized his brother only had a few chips left.

"Looks like you're out of chips, James. Lets head to the bar so we can talk this whole thing out." Zeb reached out to collect his own large stack of chips from the table.

"No!" said James. "I don't want to fold."

"All right. Want to borrow some of mine?" Zeb split his pile in two, giving half to James.

"I don't want anything of yours, not even your damned wife," spat James, pulling something from his pocket. "I want to use this for my bet." He flipped open the small box to show both the wedding rings he'd bought for his marriage.

"Whoa, that's nice," said one of the poker players with a whistle.

"What's that worth?" asked another of the men.

"James, what the hell are you doing?" grumbled Zeb. "Put those away."

"Why should I?" asked James. "I obviously don't need them

anymore now that you stole my bride." He pushed the box forward on the table.

"You stole your brother's bride?" asked one of the players.

"What a low-down bastard," remarked another.

"No, it's not like that," Zeb told them with a shake of his head. "I didn't even know I got married."

"Drunkard," he heard another of the men say under his breath.

"I'm sorry, sir, but you need to use chips," the dealer told James. "You'll have to fold and go next door to the pawn shop with that and then come back with chips."

"I might as well sell them, since they mean nothing to me anymore." James reached out for the box, but Zeb's hand snatched it away first.

"I'll buy these from you, James. How much are they worth?" He pushed half his pile of chips over to his brother. The chips were worth well over five thousand dollars and that probably more than covered the cost of the rings.

"More than that," said James, eyeing up the rest of Zeb's pile. Zeb had a stack left worth another five grand. His brother was only saying this because he was pissed at him.

"By all means, take the rest of my stack," said Zeb sarcastically, pushing the rest of his chips over to his brother. He snapped closed the ring box and stuck it in his pocket. This was a no-limit table and Zeb knew that in James' misery he had probably just pissed away more than he could afford. Zeb had money and he didn't mind giving it to James. Not if it was going to buy peace between them.

"Fine," said James, scooping Zeb's chips in front of him.

"What'll it be?" asked the dealer. It was James' turn to bet.

"I'm all in," said James pushing the entire stack of chips into the center of the table.

"What?" spat Zeb, his eyes going to the community cards and

realizing that there was nothing there worth anything other than a pair of deuces.

A few more folds came from the table except for one man who sat next to James.

"James, that's a lot of money. What the hell are you trying to prove?" asked Zeb.

"Who said I was trying to prove anything?"

"Well, I only hope you have some damned good cards in the hole to at least pull off a full house or you just pissed away a lot of cash."

The man next to James went all in as well. Now it was time to see who won. Zeb felt a knot in his stomach and almost died when the man next to him uncovered his cards and showed that he had a pair of queens and used the cards on the table to get a full house.

"Better luck next time," Zeb told his brother, knowing that James always seemed to have bad luck follow him everywhere he went. Plus, he wasn't known for making good snap decisions. Zeb had no doubt in his mind that James probably had nothing at all in his hand and was only bluffing.

Slowly, James turned his cards over, displaying a pair of deuces.

"Damn!" the man next to him swore as the dealer announced that James had just won the pot. Zeb stared at his brother's cards in awe, realizing that he won with four of a kind.

"You won? With fours deuces?" asked Zeb, still not able to believe it. "And you didn't even know you'd have a chance until you saw the turn and river cards but yet you kept betting? You pulled one of the stupidest moves ever known in poker and ended up winning."

James looked over and smiled as he collected his winnings. "Well, we both win then, don't we? I get the money and you get the girl."

Zeb didn't answer. He was feeling more like the loser right

now. He not only just lost a lot of money by giving it to his brother, but he also lost his bachelorhood. Catalina was far from being a prize of any kind as far as he was concerned.

* * *

CATALINA WAS at her blackjack table, just having started her shift when she heard the shouting and cheering from across the room. When she looked up, she saw Zeb and James sitting together at the poker table. James looked happy and was smiling but Zeb had a scowl on his face.

"What's going on?" asked one of her players, looking over toward the poker table as well.

"Herbert, let's go to the poker tables!" The man's wife came rushing over. "Some cowboy just won a fortune!"

"Let's go," shouted another of her customers and, before she knew it, the entire table grabbed their chips and headed away from her.

"Cat, can you hear me?" came the voice of her boss and ex-boyfriend, Denny Gianopoulos, over the hidden speaker in her ear.

"I hear you," she said softly, smoothing her hair over her ear and trying to look nonchalant, glad no one was at her table to know what she was doing.

"Good, then get your ass over to that poker table right away because some cowboy is walking away with the jackpot. I think it's the same cowboy that was in here last month and kept winning at your blackjack table. You remember. He's the one you were supposed to take care of, but you didn't. So now you have a second chance to make good. You know what to do."

"Crap," she said under her breath, realizing Denny wanted her to hustle James. She hated having to be deceitful. If she didn't obey Denny, he'd see to it that she'd not only lose her job, but he'd blacklist her from working anywhere in Vegas. He had connections and he had ways of getting what he wanted. Denny Gianopoulos never let anyone walk out of his casino with a large amount of winnings.

"What'd you say?" came Denny's voice over the earpiece.

"I said – I hope he doesn't go to the craps table. It's crazy that he won again."

"He's too lucky and needs to be brought down. Now, get over there and lure him back to your table and work your magic."

Denny wanted her to do something she never felt good about. Whenever someone won a lot of money in his casino, it was her job to bring the man over to the blackjack table, using whatever method it took. Denny wanted her to flirt, smile, laugh, and insinuate they might get lucky with her as she bent over in front of them letting them get a glimpse of cleavage or a peek at her long legs. Then she'd deal them bad hands by cheating, all the while coercing them to keep playing, until they'd lost everything they'd previously won.

"I don't think I'll be able to do this," she whispered, causing Denny to turn into a maniac at the other end.

"I see him on the monitor and he's collecting his winnings and leaving the table! Now get your ass over there quickly and do what I tell you, or you're fired and can go back to flaunting your tits in that dance hall."

That angered Cat. Denny knew that the reason she was fired from being a showgirl and it was because she refused to dance topless. She could never go back to dancing now. She was too old at the age of thirty, and well past her prime for a profession that was for the young. No one wanted a dancer that old, because they knew her looks were going to start to fade soon. Her body wasn't as supple as the twenty year olds'.

"Get going!" Denny screamed in her ear, causing her to jump at his bark.

"Ok, ok," she said, putting down her deck of cards and heading over toward the crowd.

Denny was slipping, she realized. Because as soon as he reviewed the tapes from last month, he'd know that the only reason James had won so much at her blackjack table in the first place was because she liked him and was dealing him good hands. But if Denny hadn't been so busy bedding all the new cocktail waitresses, then maybe he would have caught the fact she was pulling one over on him.

She wanted to leave Denny now more than ever. He had announced to her last month that he'd be marrying her sometime soon. And with him, there was no negotiating. She didn't want to be married to a man like him, but she also was afraid of being alone. Cat had worked for his father for so long that this was the only place she knew as home. She didn't want to go back to being poor and living on the streets. That's why she had made the decision to marry someone else before she ended up stuck with that louse for the rest of her life. So, she'd chosen James to be the man she'd marry. He had promised to take her far away from here and she figured she'd hide out on his ranch. Too bad that plan hadn't worked.

Cat hadn't gone to bed with Denny in over two years now. She wished in her heart she hadn't been suckered into doing so in the first place when his father passed away and the rat took over the family business. His parents, Cadmus and Sophia, were a nice old couple. They had taken Cat in with open arms at the young age of eighteen. It was after she'd dropped out of school and lived on the streets for two years after her mother died. She had thumbed a ride to Vegas.

The Gianopoulos' were the only family Cat knew out here. It was Cadmus' idea she use the name of Ebony in the casino to protect her identity from the many men who came to gamble. If it hadn't been for Denny's parents, Cat would have ended up homeless on the streets.

In the days before Denny took over, there was no cheating the customers. In the past few years, things at the Diamond Dust

Casino had gotten really bad. She didn't like doing Denny's dirty work, but until she found a way to get out from under his thumb, she had no choice. Even living with a louse like Denny wasn't nearly as bad as having to be on her own. She never wanted to be alone again.

Cat pushed her way through the crowd, hiked up her dress, and pulled down the bodice to expose a little more cleavage. Then she stepped forward to do the job she hated more than anything in the world.

"Hey there, you lucky cowboy, how about coming on over to my blackjack table for a spell?" she asked James.

ZEB'S HEAD SNAPPED UP, not able to believe his eyes or ears. There was Cat – his damned wife – smiling and flirting and turning on the sex appeal, trying to charm James into falling under her spell.

"Forget it, Cat," grumbled Zeb. "James is on to your game, so keep your spells to yourself. He's not going anywhere near your table."

"Let me help you carry all those heavy chips," she said, bending over the table to scoop them up, giving everyone a good look down her bodice at those remarkable boobs. In the process, everyone could also see up her skirt, getting a glimpse at those incredible, sexy, long legs. Zeb was getting hard just looking at her.

"Cat, why the hell are you doing this?" Zeb hissed, putting his hand on her arm.

She looked down at his hand and then slowly lifted her gaze to his. If looks could kill, he'd be dead by now.

"I'm doing my job. Now get your hands off of me or I'll call security."

"Ebony, is this man bothering you?" asked the poker dealer. Zeb could see his hand moving toward the hidden button under the table, getting ready to signal for help.

"I'm not bothering her," snapped Zeb. "She's my wife." He held up his hand and showed the man the ring.

"I've never seen him before in my life," Cat lied, putting the chips in a basket, not making eye contact with him at all. That's when Zeb realized she was no longer wearing her wedding ring. This pissed him off, but he decided he no longer cared. His marriage to Cat would be annulled soon anyway.

"Come on, James, let's go have a beer before my plane leaves," Zeb told his brother. "I've still got a few hours before I go." He tried to coerce his brother, although he knew James was still sore at him.

"No, Zeb, you go ahead. I'm going to go play blackjack instead." James headed over to the blackjack table with Cat leading the way, carrying half his chips. Zeb's money, that is.

Zeb watched Cat sway her hips and turn on the charm, realizing the woman was very good at getting whatever she wanted from men by just using her looks.

"Zeb, what's all the commotion about?" Cappy walked up next to Zeb with a little bucket filled with tokens for the quarter slot machine.

"Oh, it's nothing, Aunt Cappy." Zeb shook his head in disgust. "I just gave James ten grand and he won at least another ten. Now he's about to lose it all because of my conniving little wife."

"Are you talking about Cat?" she asked. "Because you don't sound as if you like her much. She's a nice girl, Zeb. I don't know why you two don't get along. You should try harder. After all, she *is* your wife."

"Not for long, she's isn't," Zeb mumbled. "Aunt Cappy, in a few hours I'll be on a plane back to Michigan and will never have to look at her again."

"What do you mean?" The woman's brows dipped and she looked at him suspiciously. "You're not taking her with you?"

"Why should I?" asked Zeb. "The annulment can all be done quickly and we probably won't even have to go to court. It shouldn't take more than a few weeks tops. Then I'll be a free bachelor again. Believe me, I'm looking forward to it."

Cappy hesitated for a moment but then answered. "You're leaving Vegas in a few hours? What a coincidence. So am I. I decided to come back to Sweetwater to be near all my nephews."

"That's nice," said Zeb, not really listening to his aunt, or caring where she lived. He made his way toward the blackjack table with Cappy right behind him.

"Where are you going?" she asked.

"To play blackjack," he answered with a crooked grin. There was no way in hell he was going to let James lose all his money to a woman who was about to hustle him. He realized that the only way to stop this from happening was to catch the little feline in the act.

CHAPTER 4

It didn't take long before Cat was able to start winning back the money from James by dealing him bad hands. Everyone crowded around the table watching. The only two players playing against the house now were James and Zeb. She wished to hell Zeb hadn't come to her table because it only made her twice as nervous.

Zeb was a lawyer and used to dealing with people who were lying and cheating. He probably topped the list of shady dealings with the things he'd done. But he was observant – more observant than most people. Although she was good with the slight of hand, she wasn't sure how easy it was going to be to fool him.

She took it slow at first, letting each of them win a few rounds to make them feel as if they had a chance. But with Denny screaming obscenities in her ear every two seconds telling her to hurry it up, it became very distracting. So, she pretended to be fixing her hair and she pulled out the hidden earpiece and quickly dropped it down her cleavage. Thank goodness it was a remote device and she had no wires or boxes attached, or it would be harder to hide.

"What did you just drop down your dress?" asked Zeb. She

tried to keep any emotion off her face. She blinked and pursed her lips a little.

"Please, sir, I know you've been staring at my cleavage all evening, but try to keep your mind on the game."

"Zeb, stop staring at her cleavage," complained James. "You're disgusting."

"No, I swear I saw her drop something down her dress," he protested.

ZEB WATCHED Cat shuffle the cards quickly, knowing she was cheating somehow, because the house was winning way too often now. He was sure her plan was to win back all James' jackpot somehow or another, though his fool brother couldn't see it coming.

Two cards were dealt to each of them with only one of Cat's cards face up – a ten. Zeb looked at his hand, having a sixteen already. It was going to virtually be impossible to beat the house.

"I surrender," he said, giving up half his bet rather than going bust with another card.

"I want to double-down," said James. Zeb wasn't even looking at his brother's cards because he noticed something about Cat. There were times during the game where she blinked a lot. She blinked twice as much as she normally did in her usual flirting.

Cat won another round and Zeb purposely surrendered the next three rounds in order to have more time to study Cat's actions.

Then James won two rounds in a row.

"Yes," he heard his brother say. "I finally started winning."

"Interesting," said Zeb, since he'd noticed Cat blinking a lot each time she gave James the winning card.

"James, I thought you were more of an adventurous type of man," said Cat with a smile.

"What do you mean?" he asked.

"Do something crazy like your wild stripper of a brother would do," she suggested. "Bet everything you've got on this next hand."

"Hold on," said Zeb, his hand shooting out to stop James from betting away the farm. "Brother, don't do it. She's obviously cheating."

"What do you mean?" asked James. "I won the last two hands."

"That's right," said Cat. "And three times is a charm. So make a big bet and win big this time, James. I feel like you're getting lucky."

"Don't do it, James, or you're a fool," Zeb warned him aloud. "She's not going to let you win. Let's just go get a beer now and forget about all this."

"Are you going to let him tell you what to do?" Cat asked James. "Aren't you man enough to make your own decisions, Cowboy?"

"For God's sake, Cat, stop it," Zeb snapped. "I don't know what you think you're doing, or why, but it's got to stop right now."

Zeb got up angrily from the table, watching the devious little wench as she collected the cards from the last round. He thought it was odd that she played with a single deck instead of using the continuous card shuffling machine used by the bigger casinos. Then he noticed her hand covering the ace of hearts that won his brother the last round. Her eyes started blinking a lot at the same time. Now, from the angle he was standing, he caught a glimpse of her pinky finger in the center of the deck, right where she put the ace. She pretended to shuffle, and he swore she did some kind of hand maneuver with the deck, though he couldn't prove it.

"I'll bet it all this time," he heard his fool brother spout, pushing the entire pile of chips forward. Cat smiled and dealt him two cards as well as two to herself.

Zeb walked closer to see that James had a five and a seven. Cat had a queen turned up and one card that was still hidden.

"Hit me," said James, stupidly. Zeb felt like hitting his brother at this moment to knock some sense into him. Cat dealt James a card and it was an eight.

"I'll stay," James said with a satisfied smile on his face, having a total of twenty. So now, the only way that Cat could win was twenty-one. If she didn't take a hit, she could have an ace as her hidden card.

She didn't take a hit as Zeb expected, and he quickly moved in closer as she reached to turn over her card.

He slammed his hand down atop hers in order to keep her from flipping it over.

Her head snapped around and she glared at him. "Let go," she warned him.

"Zeb, what are you doing?" asked James.

"I saw her cheat," Zeb ground out.

"You don't know what you're doing," she told him, sounding a bit panicked if he wasn't mistaken.

"I know exactly what I'm doing, and so do you. I'm busting you for cheating."

"What's going on here?" came a low voice from behind him. He let go of Cat's hand and turned to see a dark-haired man a little shorter than him walk up with two bouncers.

"This woman is cheating," Zeb told them. "And who would you be?"

"I'm Denny Gianopoulos, the owner of this casino," said the man. "I assure you that my blackjack dealer is not cheating."

"Really. Then have her turn over that last card. I assure you it's an ace of hearts."

Cat and Denny exchanged odd looks, and the crowd waited in anticipation.

"Go ahead," Denny told her. "Turn over the card."

"Denny?" Cat seemed hesitant and didn't want to do it.

"Do it!" he shouted, and she turned it over. Just like Zeb knew it would be – it was the ace of hearts.

"House wins," she said with an unemotional face, staring at Denny the entire time.

Zeb looked over at his brother and saw the despair cross his face. The realization finally hit him that Cat was hustling him all along.

"How could you do that to my brother?" Zeb growled.

"I don't know what you're talking about," she said innocently, batting her eyelashes, using those big, full lips in a seductive pout.

"You cheated," he spat.

"Just because she drew an ace doesn't mean anything other than she was lucky," said Denny. "Now, clean up the cards, Ebony."

Cat reached out quickly for the cards, but Zeb trapped her hand under his and stopped her again.

"What are you doing, Zeb?" she asked in a mere whisper.

"Proving that you're a cheater," he told her in a low voice. "I watched you, and every time you were cheating, you blinked your eyes like crazy. I saw you scoop up that ace after the last round and put it exactly where you wanted it in the deck. You used the classic pass, sleight of hand."

"I saw it, too," came a voice from the crowd that sounded a lot like Aunt Cappy's. Then another man called out that he saw it and, before Zeb knew it, the crowd started talking and getting restless. He saw a shadow darken Denny's face.

"Do you believe me now that my wife is nothing but a cheater?" asked Zeb.

"What do you mean she's your wife?" Denny's eyes opened wide in surprise.

"Didn't she tell you? We were married last night."

"Cat, is this true?" asked Denny, dropping the act and calling her by her real name.

"It is," she admitted, raising her chin.

There was dead silence for a moment. Then Denny looked out at the crowd. "I apologize for all this. I had no idea my black-jack dealer was cheating. But now I see that you all weren't the only ones being cheated on."

"Denny, what are you saying?" asked Cat in sheer panic.

"I'm saying you went behind my back and got married. How could you, after all I've done for you? We were supposed to be married, and you know it." He looked out at the crowd again. "I assure you, I'll take the proper measures to deal with this situation." His finger shot out and he pointed at Cat. "This woman no longer works here, because she's fired!"

The crowd went wild and commotion started. Zeb heard people asking for their money to be returned. He looked over at James who was not watching any of them. He scooped up his chips and was dumping them into the basket his aunt held out in front of him.

Denny took off through the crowd and the bouncers tried to control the upset people.

"Denny, wait!" Cat took a step forward to go after him, but Zeb stopped her.

"Give it up, sweetheart. It's over," Zeb said in her ear.

She reached out and slapped him hard across the face, and Zeb heard his aunt gasp in surprise from behind him.

"How could you do this to me?" Cat asked him with a tremble to her voice.

"How could you do that to my brother?" he rallied.

"Because of you, I've just lost my job."

"What a shame," he said, letting his eyes drop down her cleavage. "Well, then I guess you won't be needing this anymore." He reached into her cleavage, plucking out a small earpiece between his two fingers and then dropping it to the ground, smashing it under the toe of his shoe.

Her eyes were wide in surprise. She looked sexier than hell in her tight, black dress with her long, dark locks cascading down over her shoulders.

"What am I supposed to do now?" she asked softly.

"I don't know," he said. "Nor do I really care." He turned to go, but she grabbed his arm and spun him back around toward her.

"You can't just walk away like this. You're my husband."

"I can and I will," he told her, drinking in her beauty and watching her tongue shoot out to moisten her lush lips. "In a few hours, I'll be on a plane to Sweetwater, Michigan, and we'll never have to see each other again. The annulment is already in progress. It will be finalized in a few weeks. With any luck, we'll not even have to go to court."

"So I'll never see you again?" Her eyes darted to his mouth and her lips turned down into a practiced pout, using her seductive, manipulative charm on him.

"That's right, sweetheart, so take your last look at your husband. If you ever see me again, I'll be a bachelor. A bachelor is what I'll be for the rest of my life."

She did something next that Zeb never expected. She leaned over and pressed her lips against his in a delicious, seductive kiss. He felt his groin stir immediately. His hands rested on her shoulders and he pulled her closer. Her tongue shot out into his mouth, about sending him through the roof. And then she rubbed those big, beautiful breasts up against him as her hand slid down his chest between them, moving closer and closer to his waist.

He wanted her more than anything right now. The taste of her lips was like ambrosia of the gods. She was sweet, succulent, and all woman. His hands moved closer to the sides of her breasts. As the kiss became more passionate, he slipped his hands down to her waist and around her back side, resting them atop the curves of her bottom end. He was so hot for her that he wanted to not only bring her home with him right now, but to throw her atop the blackjack table and take her with everyone watching.

What was it with this beautiful, seductive woman that when she turned on her charms, he couldn't turn off his reactions? He felt if he didn't bed her soon, he was going to burst.

"No!" he cried out, pushing her away, gaining the attention of both his brother and his aunt. "I won't let you manipulate me the way you do all men just to get what you want. I don't care if you are my wife and out of a job, you are not coming to Sweetwater with me. That is the last place I want to take you, you devious little siren. Do you understand? This farce of a marriage is over! I never want to see you again."

As Zeb stormed away, he could have sworn he heard her whisper the words, "We'll just see about that." The throbbing was back in his head as well as below his belt. He had a sick feeling in the pit of his stomach. He just knew this girl was going to be like a bad penny and keep showing up, and maybe it wouldn't be so easy to rid himself of her after all.

CHAPTER 5

Tarnished Saints

*Z*eb felt bad about leaving Cat behind, but he couldn't bring along any more baggage on the plane without having to pay for it. He'd already paid dearly in his opinion, after giving away ten grand to his brother while trying to make amends for the whole wedding mix-up. Not to mention, getting married when he didn't want to was a huge price to pay, even if it was on accident.

He knew Denny, the casino owner, was crooked, so he was sure he wouldn't have Cat arrested or it would point a finger at himself. Being a lawyer, Zeb should sue him or report him or do something so he wouldn't get away with this. He would have, if he didn't think it would mean trouble for Cat. While she was a cheat and a seductress, she was still his wife, for now. He couldn't do that to her. Damn it, he hated the fact he'd been having second thoughts since he left the hotel, and wondered if he should pick up the phone and try to call her and tell her he was sorry for not taking her with him back to Sweetwater.

Too late for that, he decided. Besides, he didn't even know how to reach her. For all he knew, she was already flirting with some rich guy to buy her way to where she wanted to go. He sat waiting in the airport, getting ready to board the plane. His conscience gnawed at him and he pulled out the ring box from the top of his travel bag and popped it open.

"Wow, those rings must be for someone special," said the elderly man sitting next to him. "She must be a wonderful girl. When are you popping the question?"

"I'm not." Zeb snapped the box shut and stuck it back into his bag.

"Why not?" the man asked, then looked down at Zeb's hand. "Oh, you're already married to someone else I see."

"Don't worry about it, old man," said Zeb, loosening his necktie, feeling like he was being choked all of a sudden. He shouldn't have even worn the damned tie. He didn't need to dress in a suit to come to Vegas, but he enjoyed dressing up and displaying the finer things in life that he was able to afford. After all, he'd earned every bit of it himself. Nothing was given to him on a silver platter. Zeb worked hard to put himself through law school since his parents were money poor and couldn't afford college for any of their twelve sons.

He glanced at his Rolex, realizing they'd be boarding any minute. He heard the woman at the desk call for the passengers with first class tickets. He and the old man next to him both got up and got in line.

"I feel sorry for your wife," the man grumbled. "She's probably not even aware you have a girlfriend."

"I told you – don't worry about it," Zeb snarled. "She's not going to be my wife in a few weeks anyway."

"How could you?" The man made a face and shook his head.

"You have no idea what kind of girl I married."

Just then, Zeb heard his aunt call out his name and he turned to see James, Aunt Cappy and, lo and behold, his traitorous wife, Cat, hurrying to catch him before he got on the plane.

"Zeb, wait up," called out Cappy as she ran toward him, her large breasts bouncing back and forth and surprisingly not knocking her out in the process. He wasn't even sure it was safe for her to try to run at her age. Hell, she had to be pushing sixty-five at least. Then again, Aunt Cappy never let things like age or weight stop her from doing whatever she wanted. That was always one thing he admired about her. Fearless – or stupid, he wasn't sure which, but either of them had merit in her case.

"Slow down, Aunt Cappy, before you kill yourself," Zeb called out. "Now, tell me, what's going on?" He noticed that James was not only pulling a small wheeled suitcase behind him but he also had a very large bag that looked a lot like one of Cappy's old carpetbags on his shoulder.

"Wait for Cat," said Cappy, taking the carpetbag from James' shoulder and giving it to Cat. "Now, dear, you can give me the bag back next time you see me. I'll be in Sweetwater in the next day or two."

"Next day or two?" Zeb could see where this was leading. "Aunt Cappy, you told me that you were leaving today. By the way, how the hell did you all get through security without tickets?"

"I was supposed to leave today, sweetie, but I gave my ticket to your wife instead," Cappy answered with a wink of her eye. "And Cat got us through security. She has her ways of getting what she wants and she's good at it."

Point proven, Zeb thought.

"She's the wife you're divorcing?" asked the old man in surprise, looking over his shoulder. "You're nuts," he said, scanning Cat's body.

"Just stay out of this," he told the old man. The man shook his head and gave his ticket to the attendant before heading down the ramp leading to the plane. "Cat," Zeb said, looking back to his new wife. "You can't come back to Sweetwater with me."

"Why not?" asked James, handing over the wheeled suitcase to Cat. "After all, she is your wife. If she were my wife, I'd make sure she was with me wherever I went and not leave her stranded without a job or a place to live like you did."

"Well, she's not your wife, James, and I don't need you deciding what I should do." Zeb felt frustrated and aggravated by all this. Then he realized what James said and looked over to Cat. "What does he mean you have no place to live?"

"I was . . . living with Denny," she said with downcast eyes. "He not only fired me but kicked me out."

"You are unbelievable," hissed Zeb. "You married me while you were shacking up with that louse?"

"It's not what you think," she protested. Her precisely mani-cured brows dipped as she spoke. "It was purely platonic . . . or at least for the last few years, anyway."

"Your ticket please, sir. You are holding up the line." The woman collecting the tickets held out her hand. Zeb gave her his ticket. Then Cat tried to give her ticket to the woman, but the woman gave it back. "I'm sorry, ma'am, but you'll have to wait until the others board. Your seat is at the back of the plane."

"Oh," said Cat, looking up at Zeb as if she were waiting for him to do something about it.

"Don't look at me," he told her. "I'm not giving up my first class seat. You will have to wait just like the lady said. By the way, just because you coerced my brother into carrying your luggage, don't think you're going to talk me into carrying it for you when we land."

"I'll see you in Sweetwater in a day or two," Cappy called out, waving her arm in the air.

"What about you, James?" Zeb called out to his brother. "What do you plan on doing?"

"I'll be there, but not right away," he told him. "I've got to get back to Texas to collect my horses. I'll be driving to Sweetwater with the horse trailer."

"Horses? Where are you putting them, and how many?" asked Zeb.

"I've got a half-dozen I'm bringing with me," James told him. "Thomas said I can keep them in his barn until I find a place of my own."

"Who's Thomas?" Cat broke in.

"Our eldest brother," James explained. "He's got six boys."

"Oh," said Cat with raised brows. "Well, I can't wait to meet them all."

Zeb suddenly felt a pang of pity in his heart for his brother. James had given up everything for the new life he thought he was going to have with a wife. A wife that Zeb ended up with even though he didn't want her. This was the most James had spoken to him since he'd found out about the marriage. Zeb missed talking to his brother and he wanted more than anything to show him that he was sorry. It was no secret that the Taylor men didn't know how to say they were sorry. That's why they always did it in their own ways, by showing it instead.

Zeb reached into his bag and pulled out the ring box, tossing it to James. James caught it in one hand and looked over to him in question. "Did you want your money back?" he asked. "The casino let me keep all my winnings if I promised not to say anything about the cheating. I have your ten grand if you want me to buy back the rings."

"No, keep the money," said Zeb with a swipe of his hand through the air. "I don't need it." This was his way of saying I'm sorry without actually having to say it. "Get yourself a good place to board those horses with the money you can get from those rings."

A smile crossed over James' face. That, Zeb knew, meant that James had accepted his apology. "You were right, Zeb. Maybe I wasn't ready for marriage and was just rebounding from breaking up with Denise after all. I think I'm going to enjoy bachelorhood the way you do from now on."

"You mean the way I *did*," said Zeb, glancing over to Cat. She wasn't even paying attention. She was digging frantically through the carpetbag looking for something. Zeb wasn't even surprised when she gave a sigh of relief and pulled out a tube of lipstick, popped it open, and started painting her lips. She looked like she was having an orgasm with the way she formed a perfect O with her mouth.

Between that and being clothed in her tight, black dress with the low cleavage and wearing spiked heels, she looked more like a hooker than someone's wife. Especially with the gobs of makeup she wore. The worst part about the whole thing was that it somehow exited him. Damn, this woman had a hold on him and he hated the fact he felt so out of control around her.

"Bachelorhood – yeah, do me a favor and enjoy it for me as well." Zeb turned and walked up the ramp to the plane, feeling glad he was sitting in first class and she was going to be as far away from him as possible at the back of the plane.

* * *

CAT SAT SMASHED BETWEEN A HUGE, balding woman who smelled like sweat and a little bratty boy not more than six years of age. The boy cried annoyingly because he was sitting across the aisle from his mother who was busy paying attention to another kid who was just as whiny.

To make matters worse, Cat's seat was right in front of the bathrooms with a line of people halfway up the aisle of the plane all breathing down her neck. She never felt so trapped in her whole life. She closed her eyes and tried to block out everyone and everything around her, but it wasn't working.

"Hey there, sweetie," came a man's voice. She opened her eyes to see an elderly man smiling at her. He was obviously hitting on her as he waited to use the bathroom. She closed her eyes again, not wanting to deal with this right now. The fat woman next to her started snoring and the little kid kept kicking the seat in front of him with his foot. "How would you like to sit on my lap and I'll read you a nice story?"

"What?" Her eyes popped open wide at that comment and she was about to tell off the dirty old man when she realized he wasn't talking to her, but to the little boy instead.

"Ok," said the kid, and he instantly stopped crying.

"If you're good, I'll give you a piece of gum if your mother here says it's ok." He sat down next to Cat and put the boy on his lap.

"Oh, I'm not his mother, she is," said Cat pointing to the woman across the aisle.

"Thank you," the woman silently mouthed the words to the man, seeming relieved. The old man opened up a storybook the boy had on his seat and read. His voice was soothing and the little boy fell asleep after the first few pages.

"That's all he needed was a little attention," said the man with a chuckle. "My name is Earl," he said introducing himself to her.

"I'm Cat," she said with a smile.

"I remember you from when I boarded the plane. You're the wife of that jerk sitting next to me up in first class, aren't you?"

Cat recognized him now as well. "Well, I'm not sure what jerk you're talking about, but if he's six-foot-two, has black hair and bluish-gray eyes and acts like he's God's gift to women, then yeah, that's him."

"Well, you deserve someone better than him, sweetheart. Especially after what he's doing to you."

"What do you mean? Did he tell you how we accidentally got married?"

"I'm talking about the fact he's married to you and has those rings in his pocket. You know, the fact he's got . . . a girlfriend," the man leaned over and whispered. "If I were him, I'd look no further – having a wife like you."

Cat smiled, knowing the man meant well, but that he was really putting his nose where it didn't belong. She also realized he was talking about the rings that James bought and Zeb had in his pocket earlier and had also returned to his brother.

"Well, sir, if I had a husband like you," she smiled and batted her eyes, doing what came naturally when she wanted something from a man, "I'm sure I'd be sitting up in first class next to you instead of back here by the bathrooms."

"Well, darned right you would. And that's where a pretty girl like you belongs," he told her. "Now, you go right on up there and take my seat and I'll stay back here in yours for the rest of the trip. Just tell the flight attendant what you want. If it's anything that's not included, tell her to just put it on my bill."

"Really?" she asked, feeling a sense of relief wash over her. "Well, that's just too kind of you, sir."

"Please, just call me Earl. Now go on, and hurry. They were already serving the food and you don't want to miss out. They serve a halfway decent seafood salad on this flight."

"Thank you," she said, climbing over him to get to the aisle, almost hitting him with her big carpetbag that she'd dragged out from under the seat. She reached up and popped open the overhead compartment to get her wheeled suitcase.

"Son, get that for the young lady," the old man told a young guy standing in line for the washroom. The guy took it down and gave it to her.

"Thanks again, Earl," she said, hurrying to the front of the plane with the bag on her shoulder, knocking into everyone while her suitcase thumped along behind her.

"Hello, Husband," she said as she approached Zeb. His chair was in a reclining position and his eyes were closed. His eyes popped open as soon as he heard her voice. The look on his face was worth more than the ten grand he'd lost to his brother. She smiled and settled herself next to him, looking forward to the trip to her new home.

CHAPTER 6

Zeb had just drifted off to sleep and started to relax on the flight home when Cat's voice woke him. "Cat, you can't sit there. That is someone else's seat," he said, quickly raising his own chair to a sitting position.

"I know. It's mine now," she said with a giggle, handing her wheeled bag to the male flight attendant who eagerly offered to help her. "Earl gave me his seat and told me to order whatever I want – on him." She pushed her carpetbag under the seat in front of her and kicked off her heels. "Wow, it is roomy up here. No wonder you didn't want to be a gentleman and give up your seat to your wife."

"Something to drink, ma'am?" asked the attendant.

"I'll have a glass of white wine," she said, glancing quickly over to Zeb. Then she looked back to the male attendant and Zeb groaned when she gave him her best smile. "I hear you serve a nice seafood salad, so I'd like some of that, too."

"Well, we've already served the food . . . but I'd be happy to get it for you, ma'am."

When the attendant started away, Zeb stopped him. "Bring me a double vodka martini – shaken not stirred."

"Right away." The man nodded and hurried to the small compartment that made up the kitchen section of first class.

"Shaken not stirred?" Cat rolled her eyes. "Okay, James Bond."

"No, sweetheart. I'm James Zebedee Taylor, and not the singer. It would do you good to know my name now that we're married."

"Oh, stop it. You're just upset that I'm up in first class after you denied me the privilege."

"What did you have to do to get this seat, darling?"

"Nothing. Earl was kind enough to offer it since he said you were being a jerk to me."

"Me, a jerk? Hah." The attendant came back and gave them their drinks and then gave Cat the seafood salad as well as roasted hot nuts and a large chocolate chip cookie. It was followed by a hot, moist, cloth napkin.

"Would you care for a pillow, ma'am? Or maybe a set of headphones would be in order?" He glanced over at Zeb and his meaning was clear. He meant because they were fighting in public.

"No, that won't be necessary," said Cat. "I plan on getting to know my new husband on the way home."

"You're newlyweds?" The male attendant opened his eyes wide in shock.

"Something wrong with that?" asked Zeb.

"No, sir," said the man, heading away quickly. Zeb turned to see the man whispering to another attendant and pointing in their direction.

"Ok, I've had enough of this," said Zeb, stirring his martini with the plastic stick holding the olives. "Something needs to change here."

"I agree," said Cat, her eyes going to his drink. "Stop ordering shaken martinis if you're only going to stir them anyway." She took a sip of her wine, moaning her approval. To Zeb, it only sounded again like she was having an orgasm. Maybe everything she said or did sounded or looked like that to him because she was so damned sexy that he couldn't be around her without thinking about sex.

"Look, Cat, we need to stop the squabbling." He tried to make amends – at least for now. "When we get home, we're going to have to have a serious talk about living arrangements and all."

"That's right," she said with a smile, opening up her seafood salad and inspecting it with her fork. "If we're going to be living together, then we really should at least try to get along."

"Who said anything about us living *together*?" The thought had Zeb's mind racing in several directions at once. If they lived together, then that meant they'd have to sleep together. Or at least in the same house. They'd have to bathe and change their clothes together and . . . he couldn't think about this right now. "Wake me up when we get there," he said, leaning back in his chair and putting his headphones in place.

"Looks to me like you're already up," he heard her say with a giggle. He glanced over to see her staring at his groin.

Damn, this was going to be a long trip, and he had no idea what he was going to do with her once they got to Sweetwater.

* * *

CAT STRUGGLED in her high heels to keep up with Zeb as she pulled the wheeled suitcase behind her and tried to ignore the fact the strap from the carpetbag was digging into her shoulder. He led the way to the luggage claim. Zeb ended up sleeping the whole way home, probably just so he wouldn't have to talk to her.

She'd never known a man she couldn't charm before now. Zeb Taylor was one tough cookie to crack. Although she'd been trying to act happy, she was scared inside and feeling very uncertain.

Everything had happened so fast. First the wedding to Zeb, and then Denny firing her and throwing her out. Denny had been angry that she'd been caught cheating at the blackjack table. He was even angrier when he'd heard that she was married. He had thrown all of her things out into the hallway before she even had a chance to explain.

Thank goodness for Aunt Cappy coming to her rescue. The woman had lent Cat her own suitcases and helped her pack her things quickly. She'd even given up her plane ticket to her. Although Cat thought James would have wanted nothing to do with her, she ended up being surprised that he was acting more like a gentleman to her after what happened than Zeb was.

"Hurry up," Zeb called over his shoulder. "My brother is picking us up and I want to get my luggage and get out of here quickly. After all, he's taking time off work to do this."

"I can't walk any faster in these heels," she complained. "Plus, this bag is heavy and digging into my shoulder."

"Give me the bag," he snapped, snatching it from her shoulder. "Why the hell didn't you wear a pair of flats to travel in?"

"I don't own flats," she said, thankful to give him the heavy bag.

"Everyone owns flats. That doesn't make any sense."

"It makes just as much sense as you wearing an Armani suit to Vegas."

"I like wearing suits."

"Well, I like wearing heels."

They got to the baggage claim and Zeb grabbed his bag off the conveyor belt. He was turning to leave when Cat stopped him. "Wait. That's my bag right there," she said, pointing her finger at a large, green suitcase that was right next to his.

"More luggage?" he grumbled and grabbed the suitcase for her.

Cat stretched her neck to see the rest of the luggage coming down the belt. "Oh, and that one, too, as well as those two smaller ones next to it," she said, pointing them out to Zeb.

"What?" he asked with a scowl on his face. "How come you have so much stuff?"

"It's everything I own, or have you forgotten? When you think of it that way, it's barely anything at all."

"Hey, there," she heard someone call out, and saw a cop headed in their direction. She was afraid at first that Zeb was going to have her arrested. Then she saw the oddest thing that made her laugh.

The cop had a baby carrier in his left hand and a small baby was sleeping soundly inside. His right arm was in some kind of sling. It also looked as if his chest was wrapped up in bandages under his clothes.

"Judas, thanks for picking me up." Zeb just nodded since the man obviously couldn't shake hands and Zeb's hands were filled with suitcases. "I hope it wasn't asking too much for you to give me a ride since you're still recovering."

"Hey, I'm tough, I bounce back," answered the dark-haired man. "It'll still take a while to fully heal but the doc says I've come far in the past few weeks. Now, come on, let's get going before Matthias wakes up. He's between feedings and I need to get him back in time for Jaydee before her breast milk starts leaking again."

Cat started laughing aloud. The man named Judas glanced over at her and then back to Zeb. "Is she with you?" he asked softly from the side of his mouth.

"Yep," said Zeb, flagging down a porter with a cart to bring their bags to the car.

"I'm Cat," she introduced herself, since it didn't seem as if Zeb were going to do it.

"I'm Judas, Zeb's brother," said the cop.

"What happened to your shoulder?" asked Cat.

"I took a bullet to save my daughter's life, that's all."

"Wow. You are very brave."

"Just part of the job description, being the Sheriff of Sweetwater. Besides, I'd give my life to save my daughter. So tell me, did you two meet in Vegas?"

"We did. That's also where we got married."

"Married?" Judas said it so loud that the baby woke up and started crying. Judas jiggled the carrier back and forth trying to shush it, but it wouldn't work. "Zeb, you didn't tell me on the phone that you got married."

"Guess I forgot to mention it," said Zeb, following the porter out to the passenger pickup area.

"Well, welcome to the family, Cat," said Judas over the crying of the baby.

"Don't bother being the welcoming committee since she won't be family in a few weeks anyway," Zeb said over his shoulder, making Cat feel very insecure.

"I don't get it," said Judas, trying again to rock the baby as he walked but the poor child just kept crying.

"I was supposed to marry Zeb's twin brother but ended up with him by accident," said Cat. "We've filed for an annulment."

"Makes perfect sense," said Judas, making a face. They were now out in the pickup area and Cat realized they were taking the squad car to Zeb's home. The car was illegally parked in front with the lights atop it blinking.

The porter tried to fit all the suitcases in the trunk while Judas strapped the baby in the car seat in the back.

"You should have told me you needed a truck and I would have asked Thomas to come get you," said Judas, closing the car door and looking at the leftover luggage that wouldn't fit in the trunk that was stacked on the sidewalk.

"We'll make it fit," said Zeb, tipping the porter and cramming a suitcase in back next to the baby. Then with a nod of his head, he motioned to Cat. "Get in."

Cat looked at the back seat. It was made of a hard molded plastic that was used in squad cars in case someone who'd been arrested started puking or bleeding. It would be easy to clean, but looked very uncomfortable. There was a screaming baby in the back, and no real room for her to sit.

"I think I'd be better off in front," she suggested.

"Like hell," growled Zeb. "Now, take off the heels and you'll fit just fine. I'll load the extra two suitcases on your lap and we'll be on our way."

Cat wasn't going to sit in the back and that was all there was to it. "Judas, is there any way the three of us could fit in the front seat of your car?" she asked and flipped her hair over her shoulder as she talked.

"Oh, no, you don't," said Zeb, obviously knowing exactly what she was up to.

"Well, I don't see how," said Judas. "I'm sure Zeb wouldn't mind sitting in the back with the baby and the luggage and you can ride up front with me. After all, you are his wife." Judas rushed around and opened the passenger side door and helped her get into the car. As Cat pulled her legs inside, she noticed the look on Zeb's face. It was anger mixed with lust. She purposely bent over to fix her shoe, looking up at Zeb and smiling. His eyes were first on her legs and then on her cleavage.

"Damn you, woman," he growled and got in the back seat. His brother loaded all her luggage atop him. She looked up to see a camera mounted on the front windshield that monitored the back seat. She almost laughed aloud since all she could see was the top of Zeb's hair sticking up above the suitcases. His hands came out to the sides to cover his ears so he wouldn't have to listen to the baby's screaming.

Judas got in the car and checked the camera and smiled. "My grandson's sure got a set of lungs on him, doesn't he?" he asked proudly. "He'd make a great singer someday when he grows up." Judas pulled out into traffic with his siren going now, as well. He made a sharp merge and one of the suitcases slid against Zeb's chest. She saw Zeb lean over and stare right into the camera as he clenched his jaw and shook his head.

"I can't wait to meet the rest of my new family," said Cat, turning around and looking through the back divider window at Zeb and waggling her fingers at him. "So, are all your brothers like Zeb?"

"Oh, no," said Judas, "not at all."

"Thank goodness," she mumbled.

"Zeb is the classy one of the bunch and also the richest. You're lucky you got the best of the lot when you married him, Cat."

Cat was speechless and didn't know how to respond to that!

CHAPTER 7

Tarnished Saints

Zeb wasn't at all happy when Judas informed him they'd have to make a stop and drop off the baby before he took them to Zeb's condo in Benton Harbor. His condo was right by his new office and on Lake Michigan about a half-hour drive from the little town of Sweetwater. The crying baby hurt his ears and the suitcases were full of grease on the bottom, ruining his Armani suit as well as digging into his chest.

"Damn," he said, noticing that Judas turned down the road toward Thomas' house instead of toward his own cottage. Zeb reached out, managing to rap his knuckles on the window that separated the front seat from the back, trying to get Judas' attention.

Judas reached over and slid open the window, but there were still bars between them. "What is it, Zeb? We're almost there."

"Why are we going to Thomas' house instead of yours?" he asked, knowing that all the kids would be home from school since it was the weekend. He wanted to hide away at his place with Cat until he'd had time to talk to her about their situation. He had to figure out what the arrangements would be for the next few weeks until the marriage was annulled.

But now, Judas was taking them right into the eye of the storm, and his entire family was going to see Cat. He didn't know how to explain this, nor did he want to right now.

"My daughter is over here," Judas said over his shoulder. "She just got home from school and we're having a picnic to celebrate since she passed her test."

"School? It's Sunday, Judas. No one goes to school on Sunday." Zeb wondered what the heck Judas was rambling on about.

"It's Sunday school at the church," he told him. "She's actually been attending a class for teens that introduces them to the Bible. Pete started it up before he went back to Peru, and it's taking off beautifully. Jaydee got all her friends to join, as well."

"Well, hell, aren't we lucky," mumbled Zeb.

"Who are Jaydee and Pete?" Cat asked him.

"Jaydee is my daughter," Judas explained. Actually her name is Judith Delaney named after me and my wife, Laney, but everyone calls her J.D.. She likes it when I call her Jaydee though. She's seventeen and the baby is hers. His name is Matthias. Pete, is our minister brother. He's in Peru doing missionary work right now but is being relocated to Sweetwater's Twelve Apostles Church soon. It's the nondenominational church our father started before he died. I can't believe Zeb didn't tell you all this before you got married."

"Well, he's not that great at communicating," Cat said, making Zeb want to scream.

"Zeb, shame on you," Judas called back through the window. "Even I know that communication is the most important thing in a marriage."

"Really? Well, I'd think the most important thing would be knowing the man's name you were marrying," said Zeb through the suitcases. "Don't bother telling her anything about our family, Judas, because it doesn't matter. We won't be married anymore in a few weeks anyway."

Judas stopped the car in front of the house that used to be

55

Ainsely's Bed and Breakfast. Thomas' six boys spotted them and ran over. The door opened and the boys started pulling the suit-cases off of him and stacking them on the ground. Zeb slipped out quickly, hoping he could somehow keep Cat in the car and the questions to a minimum.

"Don't unload the luggage," Zeb told them. "It's going to my place, so put it all back in the car."

"Ok, Uncle Zeb, said Daniel, Thomas' eldest son who had turned seventeen just recently. "Jake and Josh, you load them back in and I'll get the baby and bring him to J.D.," he instructed his nine-year-old twin brothers.

"I've got him," said Judas, lifting the baby out of the car. It was still in the carrier that was made to strap right onto the seat. It wasn't hard for him to do that one-handed.

The door to the house opened and to Zeb's dismay, not only J.D., but Judas' wife, Laney, walked out followed by Thomas and his wife, Angel, and their young daughter, Gabby. Then he saw his brother, Levi and his wife, Candace, and their six-year-old twins, Val and Vance, who came out to greet them, too.

"Wow, you have quite a big family," said Cat, stretching her long legs out of the car and standing up on her spiked heels, pulling a wrinkle out of her dress.

"Zeb, good to see you," said Thomas, coming over to shake Zeb's hand. Levi was right at his side. All the women and kids ran over to croon over the family's first grandkid.

"Have a nice trip?" asked Levi. Then he looked over to Cat and smiled and nodded his head. "Oh. I guess so."

"Guys, this is Catalina," Zeb said, splaying a hand toward her.

"Just call me Cat," she said, flashing one of her hundred thou-sand dollar smiles. "After all, I'm family now."

"Family?" both Thomas and Levi said together.

"That's right, Zeb and I are married." She continued talking, making Zeb want to crawl under a rock and die.

"Well, congrats, Bro, you sly devil," said Thomas with a slap to Zeb's back.

"Anything to get out of having your wedding at my restaurant, I see," said Levi jokingly. "Candace," he said, calling his wife over from googling at the baby. "Come meet Zeb's new bride."

"Bride?" he heard Candace say. All of a sudden, the group of women and children shifted. In two seconds, he could no longer see Cat as she was surrounded by his family congratulating her and welcoming her to the family.

"You two will be staying for the barbecue won't you?" asked Angel. "Thomas and I would love it if you could. We have plenty of food, so don't feel like you're imposing."

"Oh, I'd love to," said Cat before Zeb could object. Cat and his sisters-in-law headed across the lawn with a trail of kids fanning out behind them.

"So, what made you decide to get married in Vegas and who is she?" asked Levi. Both he and Thomas had their eyes glued to Cat's ass as she sashayed across the lawn, almost falling as her heels dug into the dirt.

"I didn't, I'm not the hell sure, and I need a beer fast," said Zeb, heading away before he had to answer any further questions.

* * *

CAT HAD the best day of her life, being introduced to Zeb's family. She enjoyed joining them for a barbecue. She had never felt like part of a family until now. Cat had been so alone for so long, and was so very angry with what her father did to her and her mother, that she'd forgotten how to be happy.

But Zeb's family was wonderful! They all accepted her so easily and were so friendly, too. They seemed so different from Zeb, and she was starting to wonder what it would have been like if she'd married his brother, James, instead.

Then she realized that when she looked at James she didn't

feel that tingle of excitement down low in her belly that she did every time she glanced at Zeb. He was sexy and exciting. He was successful and rich. Although she hated the fact he was a lawyer, she wondered if maybe he was a lot like his brothers down deep and she just hadn't seen that side of him yet.

"Tell us about your family," said Laney, holding her grandson in her arms. Cat had heard about so many people in the family tonight that she was sure she'd never remember them all. Cat was thirty years old and knew that Laney was only a few years older than her. She wondered what it would feel like to have kids, let alone grandkids. Seeing Laney with her grandbaby only made Cat feel her biological clock ticking.

"Oh, there's really nothing to tell," she said.

"Come on, Cat," said Zeb, biting into a bacon-mushroom cheeseburger. "I'd like to know all your secrets as well."

"I don't have secrets," she said, picking up her paper cup of lemonade and taking a sip. She looked up over the rim and saw Zeb watching her intently. He'd been watching her with those bedroom eyes throughout the entire meal. If he didn't stop it soon, she didn't know if she'd be able to control herself when they got alone tonight. Ever since she gave him that kiss, it's all she could think about. The smell of his musky cologne lingered on her, driving her crazy. The way the stubble on his jaw scratched her lightly on the cheek when their lips met earlier, lodged a memory in her brain.

His kiss was intoxicating and had been more passionate than any of the kisses she'd ever had from Denny. Actually, she'd sprang to life more in Zeb's short embrace than she ever had with any man she'd gone to bed with in the past. It wasn't just because of Zeb's good looks, which didn't hurt things any. There was something inside him that drew her to him. Although she didn't realize it at first and Zeb probably didn't realize it still, they were both so much alike that it was scary.

Zeb accused her of using her looks to get what she wanted

when, in reality, Zeb did the exact same thing. He was all about being flashy, wearing an Armani suit to Vegas as well as a Rolex, and throwing around his money at the game tables and also flying first class. He liked money and the things it could buy, just as much as she did.

The difference between them was that Cat knew what it felt like to be all alone and have nothing but the clothes on her back, not knowing where her next meal was coming from. Zeb, she was sure, never had to endure anything like that. Not with being a part of the Taylor family. Being part of this family, someone was always around to comfort and care for each other. That was something she longed for and missed dearly since the day her father took her brother away and never returned.

"Well, thanks for the food, but we've got to get going," said Zeb, throwing down his napkin atop his paper plate. "Can someone give us a ride?"

Cat took that as her cue to leave also, and got up to join him.

"Hold on," said Judas, swigging down the last of his lemonade. "I've got the night shift anyway, so I'll drop you two off before I head on over to the police station."

"Thanks," said Zeb. "Sorry to cut out so early, but I've got court in the morning and I need to keep a clear head. It's a pretty nasty divorce case I'm working on." He caught Cat's eye when he said it, almost as if he were reminding her just what he was capable of, and that their marriage wasn't going to last.

"Cat, how about if I come get you in the morning and show you around town while Zeb is at court?" asked Laney, handing the sleeping baby back to her daughter, J.D..

"I'd love that," Cat answered, feeling very included.

"That's not necessary, Laney." Zeb was trying to keep her away from his family and she didn't like it.

"I'd love to spend the day with you, Laney," Cat interrupted. "I'm excited to see your new antique shop." She ignored Zeb altogether.

"Great," answered Laney with a wide smile. "Then I'll come by in the morning a little before ten, how does that sound?" Laney had brownish-red hair and green eyes and looked to be about Cat's age.

"Oh, be sure to bring her by the diner for lunch," Candace chirped in. "I'd love to show her around our restaurant."

"If you want to see the town hall, come on by and I'll show you what I do as mayor," Levi added.

"Of course, you'll want to see the police station, too. I'll give you a tour after school," said Judas' daughter, J.D., snuggling her three-week-old baby to her chest. The girl was young for having a baby. She had a crazy, rebellious look to her with lots of piercings and tattoos. "I used to work there, so I'm sure dad wouldn't mind, would you, Dad?"

Judas' face lit up with a smile. "Of course not, Jaydee. You bring Cat over and I'll introduce her to the whole town."

"Let's go already," growled Zeb, putting his hand at the small of Cat's back and guiding her toward the police car.

"You didn't have to be so rude to your family," Cat said softly as Zeb hurried her away from the crowd.

"Cat, I'm not trying to be rude, and I know my family has good intentions. However, I was hoping we'd have a little time alone before you go off and become everyone's best friend."

"You did?" she asked, surprised to hear him say this. "I thought you were trying to get away from me."

He stopped at the squad car and opened the front door for her, surprising her again that he wasn't going to demand she sit in back with the luggage.

"You're my wife, Cat," he said, almost sounding as if he were starting to accept it. "Even if it's only for a few short weeks, I'd like to know a little about the girl I'm married to."

"I'd like that, too," she said with a nod, thinking that maybe after being around his family who accepted her so easily, some of it was rubbing off on him, as well. He closed the door and got into the back seat. Cat was deep in thought on the ride to Zeb's condo that would be her new home. She was also anxious, yet nervous to spend time alone with Zeb because she was afraid that she was going to actually like it after all. But if she did, it would only be too painful when she had to give all this up in a few short weeks and go back to living on the streets and all alone again.

CHAPTER 8

Tarnished Saints

*C*at was exhausted by the time they settled into Zeb's condo on the fourth floor and had brought all the luggage inside. Judas left them, and now she was alone with Zeb.

"So, this is my place. What do you think?" Zeb closed the front door, stepped over the suitcases, and led the way to the living room. Cat followed, drinking in the beauty and splendor of the way Zeb lived.

The front room had charcoal gray couches with gray and orange pillows sitting atop a geometric patterned throw rug that covered the tiled floor. The rest of the furniture was black. On one wall was the biggest flat screen TV she'd ever seen. On the other side of the living room, she saw wall-to-wall windows and a patio balcony overlooking Lake Michigan.

The interior was one big room that opened up to a bachelor-type kitchen with stainless steel appliances, state of the art, of course. There was an island to eat at with bar stools around it that looked to be art deco, bright green, and on a metal pole that could be adjusted up or down.

"Nice," she said, taking in the interior of the room. "Expensive."

"Wait until you see the bedroom."

"Oh." She didn't know what to say about that, but followed him anyway to the bedroom. Stepping inside the room, she saw a huge bed that was covered with an ivory white bedspread. Burgundy pillows lined the bed that sat low to the ground, taking up most of the room.

"Watch this," he said, picking up a remote off the bedside table. He pushed a button and the lights went on, and with another button soft music spilled forth. "Or if you're in the middle of . . . something and don't want to deal with the remote, this will work as well." He put down the remote, looked upward and gave a command. "Jeeva, open the blinds," he said. A whirring sound was heard and, all of a sudden, the entire wall seemed to move as electric blinds moved sideways and revealed wall-to-wall windows behind them.

"Who are you talking to?" Cat looked around the room, wondering if someone else was there.

"Blinds are open, Master Zeb," came a woman's voice from somewhere. Cat's eyes opened wide, not able to believe what she'd just heard.

"You have a voice activated . . . butler?"

"Not a butler – a virtual assistant. I guess you'd say . . . a maid."

"I see. And you even named her. What will you be asking her to do for you next?"

"Oh, stop it, Cat and look at the view."

"It is a nice view," she said, walking over and staring out at the lake. It was a beautiful day and the bright blue sky was filled with puffy white clouds. Through the wall-to-wall windows, it almost seemed like a perfect painting.

"Jeeva, open the patio doors," Zeb commanded. Immediately, the clicking sound of a lock was heard and the windowed walls slid open. It revealed to her a balcony with two lounge chairs, a hot tub, and what looked like garden squares with growing flowers and small shrubs in them.

"Patio doors are opened, Master Zeb," came the woman's voice again.

"The master part has got to go," said Cat, feeling disgusted by his arrogance. "Still, this is unbelievable." She walked out to the balcony to get a better look. The breeze hit her in the face and she could hear the sound of the waves washing up on the shore from down below. "Romantic," she said under her breath, feeling happy yet sad all at the same time.

"I suppose it is." He unfastened his tie and slid it off, followed by his jacket. "Have a seat and I'll get us some refreshments."

The sun was just setting over the lake and it was making the most beautiful swirls with shades of red and orange. She kicked off her shoes and settled herself on the lounge chair. Before she knew it, Zeb was back with a bottle of chilled champagne and two crystal flute glasses as well as a tray of what looked like bruschetta atop small pieces of crusty bread.

"I hope you like bruschetta and Dom Perignon," he said.

"I . . . guess so," she answered, not knowing how to respond to that. She liked bruschetta but had never had such expensive champagne before. That champagne had to cost at least a hundred and fifty to two hundred dollars a bottle. "I've never had Dom Perignon before."

"Well, since this is our honeymoon, I thought we should enjoy it even if our marriage is pretend and won't last long." He set the two flutes down on the table and popped the cork and poured them each a drink. Then he handed one to her and held up his glass. "A toast. To the shortest marriage either of us will hopefully ever have."

She wasn't sure what that meant or if she really wanted to drink to it, but before she knew it, he'd clinked her glass and was leaning on the railing looking out over the lake. "So surreal, isn't it?" he asked. "I like living here because it makes me forget about everything and it relaxes me to be here."

"What's wrong with Thunder Lake?" She took a sip of champagne, feeling the bubbles tickling her nose. "After all, by living here, you're separating yourself from your brothers and their families."

"Thunder Lake is just a watering hole," he scoffed at the mere mention of his hometown. "Sweetwater is so small that it doesn't even have a fire department or more than one real restaurant in town."

"But it's where your family lives. I'd think family would be important to you and you'd want to be around them."

"I'm close enough here," he said, coming to sit down and helping himself to some bruschetta. "Besides, half my brothers don't even live here, so what's the difference?" He took a bite, licked his lips and nodded to the plate. "Try some. It's leftovers from a quaint little restaurant not far from here. I love bruschetta. When I was in law school, I would go into a restaurant and, since I couldn't afford a whole dinner, I'd order just this."

"You ought to make it yourself. You'd probably save a lot of money."

"Maybe." He took another bite, staring out the window again. "But I enjoy eating out. Being a bachelor, I don't have anyone at home cooking for me, so it doesn't matter."

She cleared her throat to remind him he was married now, and he looked up.

"Oh, that's right," was all he said.

"Tell me about your family," she said, sampling the bruschetta, realizing it truly was delicious.

"I thought the girls already told you everything about my family that you need to know." He settled back on the lounge chair and poured himself another glass of champagne.

"Well, they may have, but there were so many names mentioned that I honestly can't remember."

"Then let me give you the low-down, shall I?"

"Please." Her glass was empty and, in an instant, Zeb was refilling it. He pampered her instead of avoiding her and she rather liked it. She wondered what it would be like to actually be courted by him. Zeb was sure to give a girl the royal treatment.

"Thomas is the eldest of the twelve siblings. He is married to Angel. He has six boys named Dan, Sam, Zeke, the twins – Josh and Jake, and little Eli. Angel has Gabby from a previous marriage."

"Ok, that's easy enough to remember, I guess."

"Then there's Levi who married Candace and they have six-year-old twins, Val and Vance."

"Oh, so they've been married for a few years then, that's nice." She reached for some more bruschetta.

"No, only a few months actually."

"What? I don't understand."

"Levi didn't know he had kids until after he was released from prison and became mayor, but I'll let him tell you about that."

"Prison? Did he kill someone?"

"No, that was Thomas – or so everyone thought."

Cat was starting to think that maybe Zeb wasn't the worst of the lot after all. This was all a lot of information to take in and she took another sip of champagne, liking the small buzz she was starting to feel. While Zeb talked, he kept refilling her glass even though it wasn't empty.

"Judas is next in line. He's the Sheriff of Sweetwater and just got married to Laney."

"So he didn't know he had a daughter either?"

"Nor a grandchild on the way," Zeb explained. "But he's adapting nicely."

"Do any of your other brothers have kids?" she asked. "Or

you?" she added, suddenly realizing that for all she knew Zeb could have kids as well.

"I don't. And as far as I know, my other brothers don't have kids either. But with them anything is possible, so who really knows? Anyway, next in line are James and me. As you already know, we're twins. Then comes Simon who was in the Navy, and Pete who is the only one to follow in my father's footsteps."

"He's the minister and in Peru right now?" she asked.

"That's right. See, you catch on fast."

"I thought your family said something about a brother raising sled dogs in Alaska."

"Yep, that's John, and Phil is teaching in France. I haven't seen them in forever. Then there's the younger ones. Andrew is a fire-fighter. Nate, who you'll meet soon, is a musician and just got back from the Caribbean. And Thad is the baby and is still in the Caribbean with Simon and most likely getting into trouble."

"Are your parents both dead?" She dabbed her hands and mouth on a napkin Zeb had placed on the tray.

Zeb took another drink of his champagne, staring out over the water before he answered. "Yes. Pa passed away with a heart attack five years ago, and Ma had Alzheimer's and was in a home. She died just recently. That's part of the reason everyone's slowly coming home. That, and the fact they won't get their inheritance unless they move back and marry."

"Yes, that part I know about from James. That was a big part of the reason we were getting married in the first place."

"Well, don't sound so disappointed." He raised the glass to his mouth and downed the rest of his champagne. He seemed both-ered and didn't even look at her when he spoke, picking up the bottle to refill his flute. "Maybe you and James can still get married after our annulment goes through."

"What?" Her heart dropped when she heard him say that. She'd been starting to think he was accepting the fact they were married. Cat had actually been enjoying sitting here talking with him and sipping champagne. She had honestly thought that maybe they could work things out and stay married, but she could see now that the thought had never crossed his mind.

"So, tell me about your past, Cat. Or should I say . . . Ebony?"

ZEB COULD TELL he'd upset Cat with his comment of possibly marrying his brother, but he had to do something because things were going too well. She was looking more and more appealing to him and he'd actually liked the feeling of being married to her as they celebrated with the bottle of champagne.

That scared him. It frightened him more than anything in his life. He didn't want to be married and tied down to one woman for the rest of his days. He liked being a bachelor and buzzing from flower to flower, sampling the many different nectars. He wasn't going to give that up, because it was a big part of who he was.

"I grew up in Chicago," she told him. "My father left my mother, taking my younger brother with him when I was only twelve. I miss my brother, Lorenzo, very much."

"Why don't you two get together again?"

"Because Lorenzo died not long after they'd moved out."

"I'm sorry. How did it happen?" His words were sincere.

"I'm not sure. My father was very vague and never really told us the details."

"Did your father have full custody of him?" Zeb asked.

"My father never married my mother. So, I guess you could say he basically stole my brother."

"Maybe you should have gotten a good lawyer to help you out."

"My father was a lawyer. That should tell you tons."

He didn't respond to that. But now it was clear to him why she seemed to hate lawyers and probably why she hated him so much, as well.

"My mother ended up losing her job and we had no money." Cat looked down to her glass as she spoke, slowly running the tip of her finger around the rim. "After what my father did to us, we had to do whatever we could to survive."

"Like what?" Her sad story was gaining Zeb's interest.

She finished off her champagne and seemed like she wasn't going to talk. Not wanting her to stop, Zeb handed her his glass that was nearly full. She took a sip and then, thankfully, continued talking.

"My mother enrolled me in beauty contests, pageants, and anything that had to do with my looks. She always told me how beautiful I was and that she wanted me to be rich someday because of it. But the contests were expensive, and she had to coerce rich men to sponsor me. So she . . . she made the biggest sacrifice any mother could make because she loved her child." She looked at the floor and a slight tremble pulled at the corners of her mouth. Zeb also thought he saw a tear in her eye.

"Are you saying she had to . . ."

"Yes." She let out a deep sigh and looked out at the lake. "She basically gave herself to those men to get the money she needed for us to survive. In the end, it cost her her life. She ended up dying from a sexual disease."

"Cat, I had no idea. I'm so sorry." Her story sounded like a soap opera and, deep down, Zeb couldn't help wondering if it was true. No one had a life as hard as that. Did they?

"Don't be sorry. That's what happens when you live that kind of life."

"So, where is your father?"

Her eyes shot up and the look of sorrow on her face turned to one of disdain. "Six feet under the ground and where he belongs. The day I saw the newspaper article saying Chicago's most infamous lawyer, George Rudawski was killed in a car crash right after a trial, I was happy. Very happy."

"Rudawski? Your father was Polish? I thought you were Spanish."

"My mother was from Spain. That's why I don't know any relatives from her side of the family, because they're all overseas. My father's family all disowned him, or so I've been told. But it doesn't surprise me. He was – not a nice man. I don't think anyone would want to own up to being related to him."

"So you took your mother's surname?"

"I did," she said. "And I blame my father for my brother's death, no matter what happened. It is all his fault that my brother is dead!"

"Sweetheart, I think you've had enough champagne." Zeb took the glass from her and chugged down the contents. This whole story was almost too much to believe. "Why don't we get into the hot tub and just relax? I'll go put these glasses in the sink and then we'll look through your luggage and see if you have a bathing suit."

He collected everything with the tray and made his way to the kitchen. He put the things into the sink and turned around, almost falling over when he saw her stripping out of her dress right there on the balcony. Thank goodness it was almost dark out, or she'd be giving half of Michigan an eyeful.

"Jeeva, lights out," he gave the command, shutting off the lights inside the condo in order to give her some privacy.

"Lights are out, Master . . ."

"Balcony lights on," he interrupted, and the little, white party lights that lined the balcony railing turned on, giving a soft glow over her smooth skin.

"Balcony lights are activated, Master Zeb."

"Don't you ever get tired of hearing her voice?" asked Cat from the balcony. "I do."

"Honey, do you have a bathing suit in one of these suitcases?" he asked, reaching down to rummage through her luggage.

"What for?" she asked. "It's a hot tub. Do you usually wear a suit in a hot tub?"

"Well I just thought . . ." He swallowed hard when he looked up and saw her flicking off her bra and tossing it onto a chair. Then there was the sound of the water being parted as she stepped into the hot tub, followed by one of her seductive moans.

"Mmmmmm, this is nice. Come join me."

"Cat, I don't know about this," he said, kicking off his shoes and pulling off his socks as he spoke. He put his Rolex on the kitchen counter, followed by his neck chain. He tried to pull off his wedding band, but it was still too tight and wouldn't budge.

He walked toward the balcony, unbuttoning his shirt and pulling it off along the way, dropping it onto the floor next to the hot tub.

"What's this button for?" she asked, and then he heard her laughing as the jets went on and the water pulsed.

"Those are the jets. It feels great on your back." He walked out onto the balcony and saw her turn around to face him, and then make a surprised but sensual face that told him she was being pleasured and it wasn't on her back.

"Ohhhhh, these jets are nice other places, as well. Are you coming or not?"

His hand was actually shaking as he reached for the zipper on his pants. He had trouble getting it down because he was growing quickly. Yes, he'd be coming all right, probably sooner than he'd intended. "I'm . . . having trouble with my zipper," he said, realizing it was stuck on his briefs underneath.

"Here, let me help," she said, rising up in the hot tub and reaching over, exposing two beautiful rounded breasts with cute little rosy nipples. Her nipples were taut and he knew she was feeling as horny as him right now.

"Hold still," she said, reaching for his zipper, using her other hand to press against his hardness to help guide the zipper down. It released with a sudden jerk. He kicked his pants to the floor

71

and stepped out, then grabbed the waistband of his briefs and stopped.

"Cat, since we're not staying married, I'm not sure it's a good idea for us to be naked in the hot tub together."

"Oh, don't be silly," she laughed. "I'm not naked! I'm wearing my thong." She stood up to show him and slipped and fell back in the water.

"Are you all right?" He quickly stripped off his briefs and settled into the water across from her.

She was laughing, and that excited him for some reason. Her smile lit up not only the room, but a loneliness in his soul for a real relationship that was a place he didn't think anyone could ever reach. She tried to move back to her side of the hot tub, and slipped again and ended up in his arms.

"Oops," she said, her hands on his chest now, and her legs straddling his lap. "Well, what are we going to do about this?" She brought her mouth closer to his. Zeb wanted to protest, knowing she was just using her body to get what she wanted. She probably thought if they consummated the marriage then they'd have to stay married or something.

"Cat, you need to move off of me. You've had too much to drink and don't realize what you're doing."

"Is that what you think?" Her mocha brown eyes drank him in, and the little party lights from the patio reflected in her twinkling orbs. He could smell the exotic sweetness of her perfume, and it was driving him crazy. He wanted her right now more than he'd ever wanted any woman in his life.

"I know what you're trying to do," he said in a low voice.

Her lips were now so close to his that they were almost touching. "All I'm trying to do is make love to my husband. What's wrong with that?" She had that little pout on her face again. The one she used to control men.

"Is that really what you want?" he asked.

"Isn't it what you want, too?"

"If you mean, do I want to have sex with you – I think the answer to that is obvious."

"Is it?" She reached down and fondled his length beneath the water and he almost came in her hand. Then she started kissing him and his resolve gave way. The kisses between them were hot and hungry and he could see she wanted this as much as he did.

"Just relax," she whispered into his ear, letting her tongue flick out across his lobe. "This is what a husband and wife are supposed to do. We're not doing anything wrong."

"Oh, Cat, I've wanted to make love with you since the day I woke up and found you in my bed."

They kissed passionately and he reached out and fondled her breasts. She gripped him tightly under the water and arched her back, throwing back her head and closing her eyes.

"Taste me," she said, and like a siren calling to him, he couldn't stop himself. He leaned forward and ran his tongue over her chest and suckled her nipples.

CAT CRIED out in delight as Zeb suckled her breasts like a babe trying to get milk from its mother. It felt so good – so right – and she took his head and pushed herself further into his mouth. She'd only meant to tease him, making him want her as his wife and making him say he wouldn't go through with the annulment before she actually gave herself to him.

But once her body started reacting to her little game, she knew she was going to have a hard time stopping. His hand snaked up between her legs and fondled her as they kissed. She wanted him. She wanted this more than anything right now, and couldn't even wait for him to agree to stop the annulment. She pulled him toward her and spread her legs over his form and slowly slid downward.

The excitement in her belly grew and she could no longer ignore her anticipation to make love to her new husband.

"Take me," she cried out, her head dizzying either from the champagne or his advances, or maybe both. Their mouths met each other urgently and forcefully and her heart beat wildly within her chest. She could feel the tip of his manly strength knocking at her door and she was more than willing to answer it, welcoming him in.

His hands slid around her waist and grabbed her, and just when she thought he was going to plummet her downward onto him and plunge his hardened form into her for both of them to find release, he lifted her off of him and plopped her down in the water next to him.

"What are you doing?" she asked, disappointed, confused, and also frantic. She needed to feel him inside her right now.

"I'm stopping us from making a huge mistake." He stood up in the hot tub and his erection was displayed gloriously in front of her face, begging her to come to him and finish what they'd started.

"The only thing huge I see is far from a mistake." She quickly reached out for him and opened her mouth and took him inside.

ZEB GROANED ALOUD, feeling the warmth of Cat's mouth encompassing him. She looked up to him with those seductress eyes. Her lush lips were wrapped around his manhood, making him want to explode. Then she moaned and slid her mouth forward, her tongue making magic circles against his skin. He wanted to reach out and push himself into her further. He wanted to let loose and spill his seed and throw back his head and scream out her name.

But he wouldn't. That's exactly what the little feline wanted. She probably thought she could lure him into bed and change his mind about ending this farce of a marriage.

Well, she had a lot to learn about him, because while Zeb had had his share of alluring women in his life, he'd always been the one doing the seducing. He didn't like the fact she was playing her little controlling games with him, using her looks and her actions to get what she wanted. He wasn't anyone's puppet. The sooner she learned that, the better.

"No!" he shouted, causing her to pull away and look up to him in confusion. Her tongue shot out and licked her lips causing him to almost burst just at the sight of it. "Get away from me," he said softly, but she just smiled and came closer.

"Playing hard to get, Zeb? That rather turns me on."

"I mean it," he said, holding up one hand. "You can't play your little games with me and think they are going to work."

"I don't know what you mean."

"You know exactly what I'm talking about."

"No, I don't."

"Damn it, Cat, can't you see you're being no better than your mother?"

That got her attention. Her smile turned into a pout but, this time, it wasn't one of her sexy pouts, but one of anger.

"What are you trying to say, Zeb? That I'm nothing more than a whore?"

"I'm not saying that. I'm just saying that you can't use your sex appeal to control me."

"Control you? Is that what you think I'm doing?" She stood up and stepped over the edge of the tub, giving him a glorious view of everything that excited him and that he wanted right now – and also everything he wasn't going to get anymore tonight.

"Cat, come back here. We need to talk."

"I think you've done enough talking already." She picked up his shirt from the floor and pulled it on, hiding her glorious naked body from his sight. "All I wanted was to make love to my husband, but now I see that you have no intention of truly making me your wife."

"Don't pull the guilt trip on me." He hoisted himself out of the tub, as well, sloshing water onto the tiled floor. "After all, you knew all along that we both had no intention of staying married yet you purposely tried to seduce me."

She blinked once, and then twice, and he was ready for her to explode with angry shouts. But instead, she kept her calm composure and just stared at him with those big doe eyes. "Believe me, that wasn't seducing. After all, you were very willing and your body doesn't lie. I think you have a lot to learn about women."

"I think I know not only more about women but I know more about you than you know about yourself."

"That's not true."

"It is, Cat. I know that you are a woman who has always gotten what she wanted by using her looks. If you weren't sexy and beautiful and always dressing so enticingly, then I doubt you'd get anyone to do anything for you at all."

"You have no idea what you're saying. I don't need to use my looks for anything." She crossed her arms defiantly over her chest as she spoke.

"Then prove it."

"What do you mean?"

"For the next week, stop using your looks to control people. If you can prove to me there is more to you than just what's on the surface, then maybe I'll consider possibly stopping the annulment."

"You bastard! Who said I wanted to stay married to you anyway?"

"Well, don't you?"

"I may have before, but not anymore. What about you? You act so high and mighty but you are no different than what you're accusing me of doing."

"What is that supposed to mean?" Now it was his turn to cross his arms over his chest.

"It means that you use your looks as well as your money to control people all the time."

"I do not."

"Yes, you do. Look around at this apartment," she said, splaying her arms outwards, which made the shirt she was wearing open wide, giving him a glimpse of what he'd almost had. "You like to impress people with not only your looks but also your wealth and your little toys. You wear expensive suits and jewelry. You drive a Mercedes convertible and, for God's sake, your condo even heeds to your every wish just by the command of your voice. That is, a female voice and you've named her!"

Zeb didn't know how to answer that. It wasn't the same. Not really. He'd worked hard for everything he had. He didn't lure it out of anyone with a smile and a flash of bare skin.

"After all, you may have paid for all this yourself, but we both know that you did it from the money you earned stripping."

"No, that's not true," he started to defend himself, then realized that what she said did have merit. "I only paid for my schooling that way. The rest came from actual cases."

"I see." She raised her chin in challenge. "So you just flash your bare skin, smile and grind your hips whenever you need to, but all that doesn't count. I've got news for you, it's no different than what you're accusing me of doing."

"So where do we go from here?" asked Zeb, seeing that neither of them was going to win this conversation.

"I'll tell you what. I'll agree to your stupid challenge, but only if you agree to do the same to prove to me that you're not as shallow as I'm thinking you are right now."

"I don't have to prove anything." He picked up his clothes from the patio and headed inside. He could hear the pitter-patter of her wet feet on the tiled floor as she followed him.

"You can't do it, can you? Just what I thought," she said with a laugh. "You are so full of yourself that you can't even drop the ego or the glitz and glamour to look inside for a mere week."

"I know what's inside me, don't you worry about that. I think you need to look inside yourself and see if all the prettiness is only on the outside."

"Fine. I'll do it. I've got nothing to hide. But only if you do it in return."

"Fine," said Zeb, taking her up on the challenge, never being able to turn away when the gauntlet was dropped at his feet. "I'll show you that I can get any woman I want or anything else for that matter without all the glitz and glamour as you call it."

"That means you can't flash your money in expensive restaurants, or wear your Armani suits or any of your expensive jewelry either."

"Oh really? Well, then it is only fair that you can't wear makeup, dress in sexy clothes that show your legs and cleavage, or use that little pout to get what you want."

"I won't have to. So is it a deal?" She reached out to shake his hand.

He rubbed his hand over his hair, realizing he didn't want to give up all these things. But he would do it for a week just to see her try to get by without using her looks. That alone was worth more than money could buy. Since this was only temporary and he was going to win anyway, none of it really mattered. He'd prove his point and then they'd go through with the annulment just like they'd planned.

"Sure," he said, shaking her hand. She gave him that seductive smile and a satisfied soft moan that sounded like an orgasm again. He pulled his hand away quickly. "You're going to need to stop that, Cat."

"Stop what?" She batted her eyelashes.

"And that, too. Stop the orgasmic moans, the pout of your lips, and the batting of your eyes. You know, maybe we should just forget it, because I can see this is just a waste of time. You're never going to do it."

"Don't you trust me?"

"No," he said, looking at her out of the corners of his eyes.

"You already shook on the deal. It's just like a lawyer to lie and go back on his word."

Now, because of that comment, Zeb wanted to prove her wrong even more. She needed to know that not all lawyers were like her late father. "All right, we'll do it. But I'm writing up a contract for you to sign and we're going to have to have a third party be the judge. That way they can keep an eye on you and your doings while I'm at work."

"Whatever you say," she said, then reached out and stretched and yawned, giving him full view of her alluring breasts. "I'm going to bed, I'm tired."

She headed for the bedroom and stopped and looked back at him. "Are you coming?"

Why did she have to keep asking him that? He felt his groin stir every time she said it. He knew he couldn't sleep in the same bed with her without wanting to do her. And if this whole contest trying to prove his point were ever going to work, then he'd have to nip her actions in the bud.

"I hope you don't mind, but I sleep in the nude," she added with a wink and headed into the bedroom.

"Damn you, Cat," he said under his breath, wondering exactly how to word the contract that he was going to have to write up quickly.

$\mathcal{C}$at woke to the sound of pounding, thinking at first it was just her head from drinking too much champagne last night. Then when it continued, she realized someone was at the door to the apartment. She got out of the big king-sized bed, still wearing Zeb's shirt that she'd tossed on last night after she got out of the hot tub. She now regretted having had too much champagne. Embarrassment set in when she remembered exactly how she'd tried to seduce Zeb.

She looked around, wondering just where he was, then walked out into the living room and saw the pile of blankets and a pillow on the couch.

"Hello? Anyone home?" came a voice and knocking at the door. Cat probably wouldn't have answered it if she hadn't recognized the voice as that of Zeb's aunt, Penelope. Or as he called her, Aunt Cappy.

She buttoned up the shirt to hide her nakedness and pulled open the door.

"Oh, good, I was starting to wonder if you two were in the middle of making love." Aunt Cappy motioned for the taxi driver to bring her luggage into the condo. Cat stepped aside and half-hid behind the door as the taxi driver walked in and plopped down two suitcases and then went back and got two more. Aunt Cappy handed him some money and then closed the door.

"Well," said the eccentric woman, her eyes scanning Cat. "Looks like I did interrupt something after all."

"No. No, you didn't," said Cat, feeling her face starting to flush. "If you're looking for Zeb, I'm not sure where he is at the moment. Aunt Cappy, how did you get in the complex? I thought it was a secure building and that you needed a key or a pass or something."

"The doorman let me in and told me where to find Zeb as soon as I explained I was his aunt." The woman looked one way and then the other, taking in her surroundings.

Before Cat could say anything else, Zeb walked out of the bathroom with a towel wrapped around him. He rubbed another towel over his hair.

"Aunt Cappy," he said in surprise, stopping in his tracks. "What are you doing here?"

"Well, I'm glad I didn't get here a few minutes earlier, or I might have seen a little more than I expected," the woman answered with a sniff. She barged into the living room, looked at the pile of blankets on the couch, and dipped her brows. Then she looked up at both of them. "Did someone sleep here last night?"

"I'm guessing it was Zeb," said Cat, looking over to see the grimace on Zeb's face. "It probably happened after he refused to come into the bedroom with me."

"Aunt Cappy, now isn't a good time. I've got court this morning and I'm already late," growled Zeb picking up his Rolex from the coffee table and glancing at the time.

"You won't be needing that," said Cat, plucking it from his hand.

"Give it back. I don't have time for games," he said, snatching it away from her. "I only hope to hell I have a clean suit in the closet and a pressed shirt and tie."

"You won't be needing those either," Cat answered with a smile.

"Why not?" asked Aunt Cappy, making herself at home by plopping her carpetbag down on the couch and then dropping her body down next to it. She kicked off her shoes and rested her feet on the coffee table, letting out a tired sigh.

"Zeb and I have made an agreement not to use our looks or anything flashy or showy to get what we want for the next week," Cat explained.

"Hah! That'll be good," said Cappy with a chuckle. "How do you know that each of you will stick to the bargain?"

"Aunt Cappy, you can't stay here," said Zeb, but the pushy woman just ignored him.

"Well," Cat continued. "My lovely husband here doesn't trust me so he's writing up a contract for me to sign."

"That's absurd!" Cappy moved her feet off the table and turned around to look at her nephew. "If anyone needs to sign a contract, it should be you, Zeb."

"That's a great idea." Cat smiled and nodded. "I hadn't thought of that."

"Now, wait a moment, I'm not signing anything," complained Zeb, holding a hand in the air. Cat sat down next to Cappy, excited to hear more.

"Zeb also said we need someone to moderate and judge and make sure both of us stick to our bargain." Cat suddenly had a wonderful idea. "Why don't you do it, Aunt Cappy?"

"Me?" Aunt Cappy chuckled. "I suppose I could," she said, scrunching her face for a second as she seemed to consider it. "Yes." A huge smile crossed her face. "I'd love to do it."

"Ok, then it's settled," said Cat feeling as if this were going well.

"Now wait a moment," Zeb protested. "I never said I agreed to this."

"Who better than your aunt to moderate?" asked Cat. "Especially since she knows both of us."

"I don't have time for this," Zeb snorted and stormed off toward the bedroom to get dressed.

* * *

AN HOUR LATER, Cat was dressed and ready for Laney to pick her up and show her the town. Zeb had left for work earlier, wearing a suit and his Rolex and not liking the idea that his aunt was staying with them. Cat, on the other hand, rather liked having the woman around. She seemed to keep Zeb on his toes.

"Oh, no, Missy, you're not wearing that!" Cappy swiped a hand through the air as Cat walked out wearing a pair of tight shorts, her spaghetti-strap sun top with no bra, and a pair of jeweled tongs on her feet.

"What do you mean?" asked Cat, not sure why the woman seemed so upset.

"You are dressed way too sexy," said Cappy.

"Sexy?" Cat surveyed her clothes. "This is how I always dress. There's nothing wrong with it."

"No, there's not," said Cappy, reaching over and trying to pull up Cat's sun top to show less cleavage. "Not if you're trying to lose the deal you made with your husband. What is the prize going to be anyway?"

Cat really had no idea, not having thought to ask Zeb. "I . . . well . . . I guess it's that . . . we'll stay married."

"And Zeb agreed to that?" Cappy's eyes about bugged out of her head.

"We made the deal after we'd had a lot to drink. He was defending his ego taking up the challenge. If I lose and he wins, he's going through with the annulment as planned."

"Well, then I guess I'm going to have to see that both of you get new wardrobes. After all, Zeb can't dress the way he did today when he left here either. Now, don't worry, Cat, because I'm going to make sure you win."

The door buzzer sounded and Cat walked over to the intercom and pushed the button. "Who's there?" she asked.

"Cat, it's Laney. Are you ready to go or should I come up?"

"I'll be right there," said Cat, grabbing her purse from the counter and heading toward the door.

"Wait for me." Cappy grabbed her carpetbag and flung it over her shoulder. As Cappy followed her, Cat was less than thrilled.

"Aunt Cappy, Laney and I have a day planned to see her shop and the town," explained Cat, hoping the woman would get the hint that she wasn't invited.

"That's great! The three of us can do that and then we'll stop at the second-hand store before I take you and Laney to lunch. We should be able to find some . . . less sexy clothes for you and some less flashy ones for Zeb." She pushed past Cat into the hall and looked back over her shoulder. "Well, what are you standing there for? Laney can help us and we'll write up a contract over lunch for Zeb to sign. Won't he be surprised when he gets home?"

"Oh, yes, I'm sure he will," said Cat, trying to visualize herself in second-hand clothes. Then she tried to visualize Zeb wearing them as well and smiled. She closed the door and headed down the hall at a good clip. "Come on, Aunt Cappy, we've got a lot to do before Zeb gets home."

CHAPTER 10

Tarnished Saints

I t was a hot September day and Cat felt dog tired from not only touring Laney's antique shop, but also the police station, the town hall, and the second-hand shop where Aunt Cappy had insisted on buying a lot of frumpy-looking clothes for Cat as well as for Zeb.

The town was small and they walked everywhere. Laney had given them a ride from Zeb's condo that was in the neighboring town, twenty-five miles away. They all struggled with the bags, and one of Zeb's younger brothers, Nate, who Cat just met today, was nice enough to help them.

"So, where to now?" asked Nate.

"We're going to lunch at the Three Billy Goats Diner," said Laney, leading the way pushing a stroller with her grandbaby, little Matthias sleeping inside. "After this, I'll have to get back to the shop and relieve Mrs. Durnsby since she was kind enough to watch the place so I could take a few hours off. Then J.D. will be home from school and I'll have to get the baby back home so she can nurse him."

"I'm really not up for lunch," said Nate, his coffee-colored eyes looking out from over the pile of packages. He had several shopping bags looped over his arms. He was twenty-five years old and quite a handsome young man. His hair was down to his shoulders and the color was a dirty blond, so dark it looked light brown. His features were extraordinary as were all the Taylor boys, and his mouth was strong and seductive, reminding Cat of Zeb's mouth. "If you want, I'll take all these packages back to Thomas' house where I'm staying and you can pick them up later. I'm going to be jamming with the band over at Burley's later so I need to get back and practice."

"What's Burley's?" asked Cat. "We didn't see that today, did we?"

"No, and that's not the kind of place to bring a baby so we won't be seeing it at all," said Laney as they walked.

They approached the restaurant and Cat looked up to see three goats. They were atop the roof of the restaurant and munching on live grass, of all things, that was planted there. It was the oddest thing she'd ever seen in her life. "Now I know where the restaurant got its name," she mumbled.

Levi opened the door from inside, holding it for the women to enter. "Candace has your table all set up," he said. "I'm sorry I can't stay, but I did make up one of my favorite dishes for you gals for lunch. It's grilled salmon with turmeric, sautéed mushrooms, black quinoa, and steamed kale. I hope you like it. I've got to get back to the town hall for a meeting, but I'll catch up with you later."

"That sounds wonderful," said Cat. "You must be an award-winning chef with meals like that."

"Why, thank you so much. I try my best." Levi flashed her a smile at the compliment.

Aunt Cappy cleared her throat and leaned over to whisper to Cat. "You don't need to do that, as the meal will be served with or without the compliments and flirting."

"I . . . didn't mean it that way," Cat whispered back.

"Levi, is there any way you can give me a lift back to Thomas' before your meeting?" asked Nate from behind the tall stack of packages.

"Sure, Nate. But what's all this?" He reached into one of the bags and pulled out a faded and oversized woman's t-shirt. It said Lounge Lizard on it and had a cartoon character of a lizard with sunglasses lying on a lawn chair in the sun. It was a hideous light green color with pink writing. Then he frowned and looked into the bag and pulled out a pair of men's jeans that were holey and faded and looked like they should have been thrown out years ago. "These things look even worse than what I wore in prison. Are you taking them to the second-hand shop?"

"They just bought these," said Nate. The two brothers exchanged glances between them that said they thought the women were crazy.

"It's for the little competition Cat and Zeb are having," explained Cappy.

"Is this some kind of bad joke?" asked Levi with a grin.

"Yeah," said Nate. "I can't imagine Zeb ever getting near clothes that weren't designer brand. He's really not going to like this."

"You boys better get going now," said Cappy. "Nate, see if Thomas will go over to Zeb's condo and collect all his things and replace them with these."

"Now I know why we always called you Crazy Aunt Penelope," said Nate. "Thomas wouldn't do that if you paid him a million bucks."

"Crazy Aunt Penelope – that's what the Cap in Cappy stands for," commented Cat.

"It is," admitted Cappy, "even though these boys are all the crazy ones – not me. Oh, and we'll have to see to it that Zeb doesn't drive the Mercedes either. That's out of the question for the next week."

"I could use a car," said Nate excitedly, almost dropping the packages.

"By all means then, you should drive it, Nate." Cappy offered up the car like a sacrifice even though it wasn't hers to give away. "Maybe Thomas has one of those old junkers he likes to fix that Zeb can use instead."

Cat almost laughed aloud when she heard this, knowing now that Aunt Cappy was the perfect woman for the job of moderator in their absurd little contest. She just couldn't wait until Zeb got home from work.

* * *

ZEB FELT TIRED and hungry and glad this day was over. His court case didn't go as smoothly as it should have, not only because his client's wife started demanding everything under the sun, but also because Zeb couldn't stay focused. He found himself distracted every time he looked at his watch, thinking about what Cat had told him this morning about not being able to wear his Rolex.

The case finally ended in a continuance, but Zeb promised his client he'd do everything he could to make sure the man gained full custody of his child. He also told his client that they wouldn't settle for joint custody in the end.

He decided he would go back to the condo and tell Cat that they should forget all about the contest. He did draw up a contract in his spare time for her to sign, but he really didn't want to sign anything she had concocted for him. Now that Cat had pulled Cappy into this, he was already sorry he'd said someone should moderate. Aunt Cappy was as crazy as they came, and there was no telling what she would do. She wouldn't let him get away with anything; that much he knew.

It was going to be hard enough to kick the woman out of the condo once he got there, but he had every intention of doing it. There was no way in hell she was going to be staying with him, especially since he only had one bedroom.

He pulled into the parking garage, angrier than ever to see an old clunker parked in his spot. Not only that, but in his second spot was a huge van with airbrushed paintings of naked women and skeleton heads and the name Death Vices splashed across it. He didn't know what the hell was going on. With a squeal of his tires, he tore out of the garage to go and park in the street. When he stormed up to the front of the building, he saw Walter, the doorman, doing his best to act busy to avoid making eye contact with him.

"Walt, what's going on?" he growled. "There's an obnoxious van and an old clunker in my parking spots. Damn it, now I'm going to have to call the cops and have them towed away."

"Zeb, maybe you'd better just go up to the condo first," said Walt, sounding sheepish. "I swear, I had nothing to do with this." The man finally looked up and shrugged.

"What do you mean?" Zeb was already feeling his stomach clench, knowing he wasn't going to like whatever was going on.

"I'm not saying anything, but that wife of yours and your crazy aunt have this whole place turned upside down. I'm afraid the other tenants are going to start complaining."

"They do? About what?" asked Zeb.

"Just go on up and see for yourself," said Walter, holding the door open.

Zeb figured he was probably going to walk into some sort of havoc, but had no idea what he was really in for until he got off the elevator on the fourth floor and headed for his apartment. He had his key in the lock and almost jumped when, all of a sudden, loud screeching music came from inside. He opened the door quickly and stepped in and his jaw dropped by what he saw.

"Hi, honey, welcome home," called Cat over the loud music.

There, in the center of his living room, all the furniture was pushed aside and his brother, Nate, was playing his electric guitar. He had a band around him with a keyboard player, another guitar player, amps, a bunch of microphones, and even a drummer.

"What the hell!" Zeb threw his briefcase down on the coffee table and held his hands up to his ears to block the noise. Then he waved them around in the air and yelled. "Stop. Stop it already, will you?"

Nate looked up and gave the signal and the band's loud music subsided.

"Damn it, Nate, what is going on?"

"Just band practice," said Nate, looking back to the rest of his friends dressed in dirty jeans and torn shirts. "Maybe we'd better call it quits for today, guys. We'll continue tomorrow, so just leave all the equipment here."

"Like hell you will," said Zeb. "Get all of this stuff out of here right now!"

"Calm down," said Cappy rushing over from the kitchen. "Nate's going to be living here now, so I told him it's fine to have band practice if he wants."

"No, it's not fine! There are bylaws to follow living here. Besides, this is my place and I want everyone gone." Zeb looked over to Cat who was wearing the frumpiest clothes he'd ever seen in his life. She had on baggy sweats and a ridiculous faded t-shirt with Lounge Lizard written on it. She wore no makeup, and her hair was pulled up into a sloppy bun. It was far from flattering. "What in God's name are you wearing?" he asked.

The band members filed out, one by one, and Zeb slammed the door behind them.

"I'm keeping our part of the agreement," Cat told him. "I'm wearing things that are not sexy. And weren't you the one who told me I couldn't wear makeup anymore?"

Zeb ran a weary hand over his face, wanting nothing more than to sit down with a good stiff drink and put his feet up and listen to some music. Some soft, classical music. "Look, Cat, I decided we don't have to go through with this whole thing after all."

"Too late," she said, holding forward a piece of paper. "We made up a contract and I expect you to sign it."

"We?" he asked with a raised brow, taking the paper, curious now to read it.

"That's right," Nate broke in. "She wrote it along with Laney and Aunt Cappy. Of course, Judas had some input from a cop's point of view, and even Levi put in a few clauses being mayor and all."

"Seriously, Cat?" Zeb raised an eyebrow in disbelief "You had to get half the town involved in our business?"

"Not half the town," she said. "Maybe just half your family. Now here." She held out a pen. "Sign it."

Zeb read the paper as he slowly slid down to the couch, feeling like he was living some sort of nightmare and couldn't wake up.

"It says I can't wear my suits or Rolex?" he asked with a puff of air from his mouth.

"That's right. If I can't wear my sexy clothes, then you can't wear your designer clothes either."

"But I'm a lawyer, sweetheart. I have a job to go to – unlike you. I need to look good."

"She's got a job starting tomorrow," said Cappy, walking over with a bag in her hand. "Cat's going to be working at Laney's antique shop."

"Well, you've certainly chosen the right attire then because those clothes are ancient. But why bother getting a job when you'll be leaving in a few weeks' time?" Zeb didn't like any of this.

"We'll see about that," Cat said, causing him to look up at her.

Her mocha brown eyes stared a hole through him. If he wasn't mistaken, he thought he saw a glint of mischief within them. He kept thinking of what almost happened last night, and how he should refuse to be a part of this contest since he wasn't going to really get anything more if she failed and he won anyway.

He still didn't want to be married, and the only reason he agreed to this stupid contest in the first place was because he knew Cat couldn't do it. He wanted to prove a point. That, and the fact he didn't like anyone saying he used his looks and his things to manipulate people, because it wasn't true. He was competitive and always had been. When someone accused him of something, he'd go to any extreme to prove that they were wrong.

His eyes swept down the page, and he squinted since it was getting late and dark and there were no lights on in the apartment.

"Jeeva, lights on," he called out, but when nothing happened, he looked up at the ceiling. "Jeeva, open the blinds," he said, trying to get more light inside. Again nothing happened. "Nate, hand me that remote. You must have screwed something up with all these amps and mics."

Nate hesitated and his eyes shot over to Cat.

"Go ahead," Cat told Nate, nodding at him, like she had to give her permission. The whole thing seemed so odd.

Instead of handing Zeb the remote, Nate just said, "Jeeva, lights on." Immediately the lamps on both sides of the couch turned on.

"Well, what do you know," said Zeb, looking around. "I guess it's working now. "Jeeva, music on," he said, and waited. When nothing happened, Cat nodded to Nate again.

"Jeeva, music on," said Nate. A sudden loud rock music blasted from over the speakers.

"Why did you change my music?" shouted Zeb.

"Jeeva, music off," commanded Nate, and the room went silent again.

"I'd better get someone out here to fix that tomorrow," said Zeb shaking his head. "It's crazy how it's responding to your voice when it's programmed to respond only to mine."

"Read on," said Cat, pointing to the contract. Zeb looked down to see something he didn't expect to see.

"I'm not supposed to drive my Mercedes? Well, how do you suggest I get to work?"

"Thomas was nice enough to lend you one of the cars he's going to refurbish," said Cappy, placing the bag that was in her hands down next to him on the couch.

"*Going* to refurbish?" It hit him like a brick wall. Zeb knew exactly why that junker was parked in his spot now. "Oh, hell no. I'm not going to drive that thing."

"Yes, you are," said Cat with a devious grin. "And Nate is going to drive your car for the next week since he'll be living here."

"Oh, really?" He looked up at his brother who just smiled at him sheepishly. Zeb felt very hot under the collar and needed air.

"Jeeva, open patio doors," he commanded, somehow knowing by now that nothing was going to happen. Everything was unfortunately starting to make sense. "Did you want to give it a whirl?" he asked Nate with an outstretched hand.

"Sure," Nate said, his face beaming with pride. "Jeeva, darling, open patio doors."

The doors unlocked and slid open, bringing a refreshing lake breeze into the room.

"Patio doors open, my sex-stud, Nate," came Jeeva's voice over the speakers.

They all laughed hysterically, except for Zeb.

"I thought something smelled fishy and it wasn't the lake breeze," Zeb grunted. "Nate, you can't be serious. Did you really change my voice activation system to respond to your voice instead of mine? And you told it to call you – sex-stud?"

"That's no different than you telling it to call you master," came Cat's snide remark.

"I didn't do it," said Nate, in his defense. "It was Cat and Aunt Cappy's idea. One of the band members is a wiz with these kinds of things and he reprogrammed it. Cat got him to do it."

"You used your sex appeal to get what you wanted again, didn't you?" spat Zeb, looking over at Cat.

"Yeah, that's what I did," said Cat sarcastically holding out the sides of her oversized shirt. "Nate's friends were so hot-to-trot once they took a look at me in this getup, that they'd do anything for me."

"Oh. So you . . . really got them to do it without . . . being sexy?" He had a hard time believing it, but it seemed to be true.

"That's right," Cappy broke in. "And now you're going to have the same chance, because I've had all your clothes replaced with what's in that bag. Now, hand over your Rolex to Nate for safe keeping."

"I'd ask for the clothes off your back as well," said Nate, "but I know they'd never fit me."

Nate was a lot smaller than Zeb, but Zeb had no doubt that Cappy and Cat would probably be having his entire wardrobe altered to fit his brother soon.

"Cat, can I talk to you on the balcony?" he asked through gritted teeth. "In private please?"

CAT FOLLOWED Zeb to the balcony, throwing a worried glance to Cappy and Nate in the process. There was no doubt in her mind that Zeb wasn't going to go for this. Why would he? He didn't want the marriage in the first place and they'd already filed for the annulment, so he had nothing to lose. He could never give up all his fancy clothes, his car, or his playthings like his voice activation system. He wasn't the kind of guy who could survive without his looks or his toys. She knew she could win this contest hands down, but Zeb was probably going to try to talk her out of the whole thing now.

"What is it?" she asked when they got to the balcony. He

looked damned good in his suit and tie with his black hair slicked back with gel. He had a few stray pieces falling over his forehead and it looked impeccable as always. He held the contract in one hand along with the pen and with the other he loosened the knot on his tie.

"You know this isn't fair. I have a business to run," he told her. "I have my own law firm now and respectable clients."

"If you have your own law firm then I guess you can wear whatever you want, can't you?" she asked.

"I'm in the middle of an important case. I can't show up one day in a suit and the next in a pair of jeans. At that rate, my client will never get full custody of his kid. I have a reputation to uphold."

"Not my problem. Besides, as far as I'm concerned, no man should take a child away from his mother. If you're such a good lawyer then it shouldn't matter what you wear, should it?"

"This game has gone too far. I'm not going to sign this contract, nor are you going to be walking around here looking frumpy anymore. Now be a good girl and go put on some makeup and a nice dress and I'll take you out for a seafood dinner and a bottle or two of wine."

"No." She shook her head and crossed her arms over her chest, thinking how disappointed she was with him. "I knew you'd try to back out of this because you know as well as I that you can't do it. You accuse me of using my looks to get what I want but, in reality, the thing that bothers you the most about me is what really bothers you about yourself."

"That's ridiculous and makes no sense at all."

"I don't know why I even thought this marriage could work. I am sorry for the mix-up and that I didn't marry your brother like I'd intended. James is real. He's not pompous and full of himself like you. He knows how to treat a woman the way a woman wants to be treated."

"What's that supposed to mean?" The look on his face told her he didn't like the fact she was saying James was better at something than he was.

"It means you think I'm a whore because that's all you know," she spat. "You shake your body and grind your hips to impress girls and get what you want and think nothing of it. Then you show off with all your fancy gadgets and devices, and driving your expensive car, and you think that you're better than everyone."

"That's not true."

"I don't know why I thought you would do this. I was just kidding myself I guess, thinking you had something inside that wasn't as showy and as fake as the outside. You disgust me, Zeb Taylor, and I no longer want to be married to you. So forget the contest and forget the whole damned marriage. I could never, and I repeat never, be married to someone like you!"

ZEB JUST STOOD THERE with nothing to say as Cat stormed away. If he wasn't mistaken, he thought he heard her whimper. And when the door to the bedroom slammed shut, he figured she was in there crying.

He didn't like to see a woman cry. Never had he made any woman cry in his entire life. He was the one who made them smile. Zeb made them feel special by wining and dining them. He romanced them and gave them shiny baubles and took them fancy places and treated them like queens.

Suddenly, he realized that maybe he had only been doing it to get what he wanted. That is, to get them into bed. Whenever he got drunk and started stripping, that probably wasn't a very respectable thing to do either.

He'd been proud of himself and everything he'd accomplished – up until now. He thought about the horrible story that Cat had told him about her childhood and what she'd gone through. He couldn't even imagine how much pain and abandonment she must have felt. After all, he'd always had his brothers around to talk to or to go to when he was in trouble. Cat had been on her own from a very young age. If they split up, she'd be all alone again.

He liked Cat a lot, although he didn't want to admit it. She was the only woman who had ever challenged him like this, and that was something he more than respected.

She was smart and pretty and very sexy, even when wearing frumpy clothes and without wearing a drop of makeup. Maybe he should give this whole thing a chance. For Cat's sake. After all, she seemed to accept the challenge and be embracing it fully. If she could do it, then so could he. He took it as a challenge to prove to her that he wasn't the louse she thought he was after all.

He walked off the balcony and into the living room where Nate and Cappy were sitting there in silence. They both looked up and waited for him to speak. Zeb sank down on the couch next to his brother.

"Zeb, I don't blame you for not wanting me to drive your Mercedes," said Nate apologetically. "I swear, it wasn't my idea to move in here and kick you out either."

"Kick me out?" This was news to him.

"Well, Zeb, if you and Cat are going to do this right, you really can't be living in a half a million dollar condo now, can you?" asked Cappy. "I figured Nate could live here for the next few weeks and you and Cat could live in one of the cabins on Thunder Lake."

"No," he said, shaking his head, fear coursing through his body by the suggestion. "Those are only for . . ." Suddenly he realized she was right. The cabins were for each of the Taylor boys when they got married, and Zeb was married. For now, anyway.

"You're married," Nate reminded him. "You might as well take advantage of it and get your inheritance. After all, I wish I could get mine."

"Then maybe you should marry Cat," he mumbled.

His brother's eyes lit up at the suggestion. "You think so?" he asked anxiously.

Zeb scowled at him and shook his head. Nate was only twenty-five and lived the vagabond life of a musician. Cat was thirty. Although she'd had a hard life, she was used to class and elegance now and he wanted to make sure she got it.

"No, I don't think so, you fool," said Zeb, reaching out and swiping his hand over Nate's head to ruffle his hair the way he used to do when Nate was just a child. "I know you're probably pissing your pants to even think about having a woman like Cat. But you, little brother, wouldn't know what to do with her if you had her. She's more woman than you could ever handle."

"A little more than you're used to also," said Cappy sarcastically.

"Not true," said Zeb with a confident smile. "There is no woman on this green earth that I can't handle."

"Then sign the contract," Cappy challenged him. "Move to the lake with Cat for the next week and see this through."

"What happens when the marriage is annulled in a few weeks and we're not married anymore?" asked Zeb. "Pa stated in his will that we had to stay married a year in order to keep our inheritance."

"My brother, Webster, wanted to see all his boys married and with lots of children," said Cappy. "You know, he always thought I was a failure since I never had kids."

"Why didn't you?" Nate asked.

"That's right," said Zeb. "After all, if I'm not mistaken, you've been married more times than Zsa Zsa Gabor."

"Not as many, but there have been a few," said Cappy. "Do you boys want to know the truth? I'm not able to have children. Most of my marriages broke up because of it. There are a lot of good men out there who want a wife and family and would give anything at all to get it. So if you don't want Cat, Zeb, then maybe you're right. You should just forget this whole contest and let her go. Let her find a man who will take care of her and treat her the way she deserves. Because after what she's been through in the past, she doesn't deserve your shit."

"Cappy, that's not like you to swear," said Zeb, surprised at his aunt's foul language.

"Oh, I swear more than you think," she assured him. "I just never did it around your father because I didn't want him forcing me to go to confession. Now make up your mind, Zeb. Either sign the contract and go through with the contest and see where it ends up with the two of you, or call it quits right now and let someone else have that wonderful woman."

Zeb's aunt was more conniving than both him and Cat put together when she wanted something. He wasn't quite ready to give up Cat yet. The thought of her making love to anyone else but him – especially if it was Nate or James, made him crazy.

He put down the paper and quickly scribbled his signature before he had a change of heart. Then he pushed it over to his aunt. "There," he said. "It's signed."

"Great. Now just give Cat your contract and she'll sign it, too," said Cappy.

Zeb opened his briefcase and pulled out the contract, thinking of how much he was going to miss Cat wearing makeup. He liked seeing her cleavage and her cute little butt in her tight pants. Just the thought had him wanting to go to her right now.

"I don't think it's necessary that she signs this," he said, folding the paper in half. But before he could put it back, it was ripped out of his hand. He looked up to see Cat standing next to him with fire blazing in her eyes.

"Give me the pen," she said in a low, steady voice.

"Cat, you really don't have to –"

"I said, give me the damned pen."

"All right, already," he said, handing her the pen. She knelt down and started to sign it atop the coffee table without even looking at it.

"Don't you want to read it first?" he asked. "It's always a good idea to read anything that you're signing."

"It doesn't matter," she said, scribbling her signature across it and dotting her I and crossing her T with more force than was necessary. "Whatever you throw at me, I can handle." She handed him the signed contract and pointed to the bag next to him on the couch. "Now, change out of those clothes. If I'm going to look like a hillbilly then so are you."

He reached over and peered inside the bag, realizing it was a bunch of old clothes from the second-hand store that he wouldn't be caught dead wearing. He closed his eyes and let out a deep breath, wondering how the hell he was going to win any case in court dressed like a clown.

When he opened his eyes, Cat was smiling at him. It was part happy and part vengeful, but it excited him either way. He loved when she smiled because she looked so sexy, even without makeup or dressed only in old clothes. He felt his lower body responding to her again and he cursed himself.

Why the hell hadn't she read the contract before she signed it? If she had, she never would have agreed to one of the clauses. It was the clause he was totally regretting putting in there right now. That clause said there would be no sexual interactions of any type between them for the next week. Not even a hug or a kiss!

Damn, he wondered how the hell he was going to go a whole week living with her without even touching her. It was a horrible situation to be in, but only he was to blame.

CHAPTER 11

*C*at had shared the king-sized bed in Zeb's apartment with Aunt Cappy that night, and Zeb slept on the couch while Nate crashed on the floor. She knew this would be the last night they spent in this luxurious apartment. She was really going to miss it. Even though she'd lived with nothing and even on the streets at one time in her life, she'd learned to enjoy the finer things after being taken in by the Gianopoulos family.

She heard Zeb in the other room moving around, so she quickly got up and pulled on her second-hand clothes and opened the door to see him standing in the living room in just his skimpy briefs. He was digging through the paper bag looking for something to wear. His eyes shot up and interlocked with hers. Frustration painted his face.

"What's the matter?" she asked. "Don't the clothes fit you?"

"Not unless you're getting ready for a flood." He held up a pair of pants that were two inches too short. After throwing them down in disgust, he pulled out a short-sleeved blue jean shirt and crinkled his nose at it. "Were these things even washed?"

"I don't know. Probably," she said, not having really thought about it, nor did she care. "When I lived on the streets, I wore the same clothes for a month without washing them, so just suck it up and put them on and stop complaining."

When he shot her a look of despair, she could see the sadness in his bluish-gray eyes. She knew this whole contest was hurting him more than her, but she'd never had pity for anyone in her life and she wasn't going to start now.

"Do you have court today?" she asked.

"Thankfully, no. I was able to juggle some things around so I don't have to go in looking like the court fool." He finally decided on a pair of khaki shorts with big, wrinkled pockets on the sides. The shorts fit, but were old and very short, ending above his knees. He pulled out a white Diego-tee next and put it on. It was tight and she noticed how his six-pack abs showed through the cotton.

"See, that's not so bad now," she said, holding back her laugh as she watched him put on the blue jean shirt over it.

"I'll die if any new clients show up in my office. Thank goodness, I have a light load this week. I'm basically still getting organized after the move. I've got a ton of papers I need to file."

"Well, let me come with you and I'll help."

"No. There's nothing you can do. Go with Laney to the antique shop. That's more your speed."

"More my speed?" She couldn't believe he actually just said that. "What do you mean by that?"

"I just meant that I know you never even finished high school. Because of what happened to your mother and all. It's understandable that you don't have any schooling, and I'm not holding it against you. Maybe if the job with Laney doesn't work out, you can go over to the restaurant. I'm sure Candace could use another waitress."

"You never cease to amaze me with the way you can be so insensitive. You know nothing about me, Zeb Taylor, so don't pretend you do."

"Well, I'd love to stay and chit-chat but I've got to get to the office." He went to grab his Rolex from the table, but Cat cleared her throat and he gingerly placed it back down.

"Oh, that's right." He flashed her one of his million dollar smiles. "Well, have a great day and I'll see you tonight." He went for the keys for his Mercedes next, but Cat cleared her throat again.

"Your new keys are in the ignition of the car," she said. "It's not locked."

"Of course not, because no one in their right mind would think of stealing that hunk of junk," he grumbled, grabbing his briefcase and heading out the door.

"What's all the noise about?" came Nate's voice from the floor. He sat up and rubbed his eyes and yawned.

"Nate, can you give me and Aunt Cappy a ride to town?" Cat asked him.

"Sure," he said slowly, then his eyes focused on the keys to Zeb's Mercedes. "Oh, right! No problem." He jumped up and grabbed his clothes and headed for the bathroom. "Just give me a minute."

"Cat?" came Aunt Cappy's voice as she walked out from the bedroom. "Where's Zeb?"

"He went to work."

"I should have been up to make sure he didn't wear any of his designer clothes."

"Oh, believe me," she said with a smile, "I made sure he didn't. Cappy, I didn't like the way he insinuated I could only hold on to mindless jobs since I never finished high school."

"Oh, don't listen to him, sweetie. He always thought he was better than the rest of the boys since he's had the most schooling."

"He doesn't know me, though he thinks he does. I'm smarter than he gives me credit for. The part he doesn't know is that before I had to drop out of high school, I was not only a straight A student, but there was talk I might someday be slated as valedictorian of our senior class. I even went to state finals and helped our school win second place in their math competition."

"Really?" asked Cappy, sounding impressed. "Well then, I think we'll just have to take a pass on that job with Laney for now, and get you something that will impress even the most judgmental of men like Zeb."

"What could I possibly do?"

"You might want to come with me to Burley's Bar later," said Nate, walking out of the bathroom having overheard their conversation. "Burley is in a big mess with the books. He's been looking for an accountant to help him straighten out the whole thing."

"Well, I've never done anything like that before," said Cat, looking over to Cappy.

"This is perfect," said Cappy, clapping her hands together excitedly. Cat wasn't sure she wouldn't be jumping up and down next. "We'll show Zeb that you can match him in anything he does."

"I can't go in there for a job looking like this," said Cat, pointing to her t-shirt and sweats.

"No, you're right. That'll never do." Cappy put a hand to her chin in thought. "I think there was a dress in that bag of clothes we bought, wasn't there?"

"There was," said Cat, "but it is the ugliest thing I've ever seen." She dug it out and held it up. It was orange with loud, large flowers on it and ended just above the knee.

"We'll just make a few changes to it, shall we? After all, we wouldn't want Zeb to accuse you of being too sexy since it's so short."

"Believe me, this is not sexy," Cat said with a sigh.

Cappy walked over to the coffee table to get her carpetbag and dug inside. She kept talking while she looked for whatever it was she needed. Her head went down into the big bag and Cat could barely hear her.

"Ah, here it is!" She held up a small box. "I brought my sewing kit."

"You know how to sew?" asked Cat, impressed since she couldn't even sew on a button, nor did she want to.

"I'll have you know when the boys were young, I sewed most of their clothes since their father was a minister and didn't have a lot of money for things like that. Don't you remember, Nate?"

"I remember," Nate grumbled. "Homemade hand-me-downs. After ten brothers wearing them first, I can't say they were anything exciting by the time they got to me and Thad."

"Come on, Missy, I'll work my magic," said Cappy, pulling her across the room. "Then Nate can take us over there and we'll see if we can get you a job as an accountant at Burley's."

ZEB CLOSED up his office early to head back to Thunder Lake. He was starved and wanted to go out to one of his favorite restaurants for some bruschetta and maybe a filet mignon, but didn't want to be caught out in public wearing these clothes. Besides, spending money in fancy restaurants wasn't allowed for the next week.

It was already bad enough that he'd made quite an entrance parking in front of his office with the car he was driving smoking from under the hood and rattling like crazy. He prayed he'd make it back to Thunder Lake so he could have Thomas take a look at it before it fell apart. Maybe he'd borrow a few clothes from him too since they wore the same size. While Thomas didn't wear anything that Zeb would say was close to being respectable, at least he'd have clothes that looked like they weren't from the 1970s. Or at least, he hoped.

He hurried to the car, trying to hide behind his briefcase, hoping no one would recognize him. He walked quickly with his head down, not making eye contact with anyone. He was just starting to think he'd made it, and had his hand on the door handle when a voice behind him made him freeze.

"Zeb, is that you?"

He turned around to see Melody Jenkens standing there with one of her friends who he remembered was called Jenny or Ginny, or something like that. These were two of the hottest girls in the Benton Harbor area, and he'd dated both of them at least once or twice. He turned around and smiled and instantly went into one of his bachelor modes.

"Melody, Ginny, wow, you're both looking good as usual. It's such a surprise to see you."

"It's Jenny," her friend corrected him.

"What's this?" asked Melody, looking perplexed when she saw his clothes. "You said you were taking us both to lunch today. That's why we're here."

"I did?" Oh, crap, now he remembered. He'd made these plans weeks ago and was going to take them both to lunch and had hoped to get lucky by having a threesome afterwards. He'd never done anything like that before, but it was the girls who suggested it, and he had been elated that they came up with the idea.

"You promised to show us your apartment," said Jenny, talking in a sultry voice. "You know, the one with the hot tub and the king-sized bed."

"Oh, that's right," he said and dragged a hand across his hair, his fingers getting tangled in a knot since Cappy and Cat had hid his hair gel and he hadn't even been able to use that.

"What are you wearing?" asked Melody. She started laughing. "You look like you're going to a fishing hole or maybe on a safari." They both started laughing at him then, and he felt like crawling under a rock.

Both the girls wore tight, low-cut dresses and high heels.

"I'm going to have to postpone the date for a week or two," he said, turning around quickly. "Sorry, girls, but I've got to go." He jumped into the car and started the engine and it backfired, sounding like a shot. The girls both jumped. He rolled down the window – crank style – and tried to flash them one of his smiles that usually made everything all right, but it didn't work.

"Where's your Mercedes?" asked Jenny, looking very upset.

"Oh, I lent it to my brother, but I'll have it back in a week. I know I promised you both lunch and a tour of my condo, but it'll have to wait. Sorry."

"Don't bother," said Melody, putting her nose in the air. "I think we're busy then anyway."

"I'll call you," he shouted out the window as they walked away. Jenny looked back over her shoulder and said something he didn't want to hear.

"We don't date liars," she spat. "You told us you were a lawyer with a penthouse and that the Mercedes was yours. Get a life, loser."

He watched the girls walk away and felt like screaming. He *was* a lawyer with a penthouse and a Mercedes. He was high class. He wasn't a loser, but it was too late to explain it. He would never be able to convince them of anything now that they'd seen him like this.

He jammed the car into reverse and it sputtered and almost died before he hit the gas. It jerked forward so hard it almost gave him whiplash. Angrily, he beelined it for his brother's house. He would have to think of some way to get Cat to agree to end this absurd contest because he wasn't going to live like this any more.

* * *

CAT FINISHED up crunching some numbers for Vincent Burley, seeing now that the man was in worse shape than he'd thought. He'd hired Cat on Nate's recommendation, but was hesitant to do so. He told Nate behind her back that since she'd come in for the job looking so frumpy, he'd wanted to dismiss her without a second thought.

It pained Cat to hear this. Even though Cappy had tried to fix up the monstrosity she was wearing by sewing on some lace and even a bow in the back, she still looked like she belonged in some 1970s sitcom. She didn't like feeling this way, and she realized that if it weren't for Nate, she wouldn't have this job right now even though she was more than able to handle it. However, without even a high school diploma, people wouldn't take her seriously.

Cat walked out from the back room and into the bar area to hear Nate and the band practicing. There were a few patrons there, but not much was going on so early in the day. She could see that if Burley had a lunch crowd then maybe he'd be able to make ends meet. However, she didn't want to suggest it, because she knew it would take business away from Candace and Levi at the Three Billy Goats Diner. She couldn't do that to them. They'd been so kind to her and she always repaid kindness with kindness in the end.

"So, what's the verdict?" asked Burley in his gruff voice, sucking on a cigar and almost making Cat gag from the stench. She had never gotten used to people smoking. But at least in the casino, cigars had not been allowed.

"Mr. Burley, I'm still going over some of the books and it'll take a while to organize everything, but it seems as if your business is in serious trouble," she told him.

"How much trouble are we talking here?"

"Enough that if you don't bring in more revenue soon, you're going to have to close within the next month."

"Shit, I can't do that. I'll have to hire more dancers." He puffed furiously on his cigar.

"Dancers?" she asked, realizing she could be the answer to some of his problems. "I worked as a Vegas dancer a long time ago, and I know all about the entertainment industry. Maybe I could help you out."

"You?" He looked at her and laughed. "Honey, I don't think you have what it takes."

"I bet you'd be surprised," she said. "I know a few tricks that I might be able to share with your girls. I also know a woman who sews, so maybe we could come up with some good costumes."

"Costumes, yeah the girls need to play some new roles," he said with a nod. "The guys are getting tired of the same old thing every night."

"I could come up with a new, exciting act that'll pull in people from towns around."

"New? Now that's something we could use around here. Okay, come back tonight and I'll introduce you to the girls." He looked her up and down. "Maybe frumpy will be a good hook, so we'll try it."

"I assure you, Mr. Burley, I am not really frumpy under these clothes."

"That's what I'm counting on, honey. You come back tonight and show me what you've got."

"I'll do that," she said with a smile, thinking it was getting easier to get a job without having good looks and dressing sexy. This would prove it. She was excited about it but she wouldn't tell anyone about this yet. She'd wait until she met the dancers and came up with a plan and then she'd surprise Zeb by showing him exactly what she could do. Cat smiled to herself, thinking how surprised Zeb was going to be when he found out about both of her new jobs.

CHAPTER 12

"Zeb, what did you do to my car?" asked Thomas, ducking his head under the hood of the bright orange 1969 Charger with a wrench in his hand.

"I didn't do anything! The thing just started back talking. Damn, I miss my Mercedes," said Zeb, walking over to the fridge in Thomas' pole barn and pulling open the door and scanning the contents. After the day he'd had, he needed a glass of dry wine or a Belvedere martini. Or better yet – some Remy Martin cognac.

He knew he wouldn't find any of that here, so he only hoped for a bottle of imported beer. His hopes were dashed when he found nothing but lemonade and iced tea. "Don't you have anything harder than lemonade?" he grumbled. "I'd even go for a lite beer right now."

"You know I don't drink anymore, Zeb. I haven't touched a drop since all my problems were finally cleared up with the murder."

"Oh, that's right," he said, deciding on a lemonade and closing the fridge, twisting off the top of the bottle.

"Speaking of problems, how are things between you and

Catalina? Are you still being stubborn and going through with the divorce?"

Zeb took a swig of lemonade and settled himself on Thomas' swivel desk chair. "Yes, and actually it's not really a divorce since we never consummated the marriage, so we're calling it an annulment."

"You what?" Thomas stood up so quickly that he hit his head on the hood of the car. "You're saying you never made love to Catalina? What's the matter with you, Brother? That girl is a sex bomb waiting to explode. You're the one in the family who usually takes a woman to bed first and asks questions later, if you even ask at all."

"Well, we just didn't. Don't forget, she tricked me into getting married in the first place."

"Oh, I get it." Thomas grabbed a rag and wiped the grease off his wrench. "She didn't want you. I can't say I'd blame her if you've been dressing like that."

"That's not the case. We almost made love but I stopped it. And I'm only dressed like this because I'm trying to prove to Cat that I don't use my looks or my wealth to get things the way she uses her sex appeal to get men to give her everything she wants."

Thomas chuckled and dug through his tools and selected a screwdriver and bent back under the hood of the car. "How's that working out for you, little brother?"

"Well . . . it's not. I saw a couple of hot girls I was planning on hopefully having a threesome with today and they basically snubbed me because of my clothes and that old bucket of bolts I was driving."

"So, maybe Cat is right and you do use your looks and wealth to get what you want from people?"

"Quit sounding like the wise old brother, Thomas." Zeb chugged down the rest of the lemonade and tossed the bottle into the trashcan next to the desk with a loud clank. "I'm sure it was only because I hesitated and postponed the date, or they wouldn't have blinked an eye at me."

That got Thomas laughing so hard that he almost dropped his screwdriver. He stood up and shook his head. "You are so full of crap that I'm surprised your eyes haven't turned brown by now," he said. "What are you doing postponing dates for threesomes? Zeb, you're an idiot. You're a married man now."

"No, not really, and not for long."

"If it's not real then why did you file for an annulment?" asked Thomas.

Zeb was quiet, knowing that he didn't have a leg to stand on where this was concerned.

"You really want to bed these other two girls when you won't lay a finger on your own wife? You're not fooling anyone. It's obvious that you don't want to change and are scared of turning the page. Whether you want to admit it or not, Cat was exactly right about you. Without your looks and your money and all your toys, you're nothing, Zeb."

"That's a crock," Zeb ground out, standing up quickly. "I think this stupid game we're playing has gone too far. I'm not going to wear these clothes anymore nor am I going to drive that old car. I want my old life back. I don't know why I even agreed to Cat's little game in the first place."

"Cat's game? I thought you said the whole thing was your idea."

"Well, I guess it was, but I meant for her to do it. I never intended on being dragged into this mess."

"I've never known you to be a quitter when it comes to a competition, Zeb. I think your ego just can't handle the fact that you are no different than what you're accusing her of being."

"She uses her sexuality to get what she wants. That's different."

"What's different?" asked Cat, walking into the barn with Cappy right behind her.

"Nothing," said Zeb, hoping Cat hadn't heard a word he'd said. "So, how'd your little job go today at the antique store?"

"Little job?" she raised an eyebrow at him.

"Cat has a new job," said Cappy, taking the seat that Zeb had just vacated.

"Oh, so you got a job waitressing? Good for you." Zeb hoped they'd given her a uniform so she didn't have to wear that godawful dress in public.

"No, for your information, I am a private accountant," Cat answered smugly.

"Accountant?" asked Thomas with a low whistle. "That's impressive."

"For who?" asked Zeb with a half-smile on his face, thinking she was just joking.

"For Burley."

"Burley?" both Thomas and Zeb said at the same time.

"That's right," Cappy answered. "Nate suggested her for the job."

"Cat, what were you thinking?" asked Zeb. "You can't work for a man like that."

"I can, and I am. And I'll have you know that I got the job without using my – sex appeal – as you call it."

"Zeb, you'd better tell her already," said Thomas, hating Burley's strip joint more than anyone after what he went through with his last wife.

"Honey, do you know what kind of a place Burley's is?" Zeb asked her, finding this whole thing amusing.

"I know exactly. It's a failing bar and that's why I'm going back there tonight to help out. If they don't do something fast, he's going to lose the place."

"I hope he does lose it," came Thomas' disgusted reply. "I've been trying to get Judas to close that place down for awhile now, but he just won't do it."

"It's where Nate's playing with his new band, so you all should be happy I'm trying to help Burley save it," continued Cat.

"You're not going back there," said Zeb. "I won't allow it."

She looked up to him and raised her brows. "You what?" she blinked a few times, and her lush lips were set firm as her sexy eyes drilled into him.

"I'm not letting you work there, Cat, so just ask Laney for your job back at the antique store."

"Zeb Taylor, I do believe you are jealous that I got a job using my brain instead of my body. You have no control over what I do, so don't bother trying to talk me out of it. I'm going to go to Burley's to work tonight, and you can't stop me."

"Think about this, Cat. What kind of guy wants a woman to come look at the books at night?"

"For your information, I'm talking about my second job at Burley's. I'm going to be in charge of the dancers."

"You're what?" This time, Thomas, Zeb, and Cappy all spoke at once.

"You heard me. I'm going to show his dancers a few new tricks. He put me in charge of the show. Aunt Cappy, I was hoping you could maybe sew up some killer costumes for the girls."

"Honey, I don't think those girls really need costumes," said Aunt Cappy.

Zeb loved how naïve Cat was, and it made him attracted to her even more. He knew he should tell her exactly what she'd agreed to, but didn't have the heart to do it just yet when she was so proud of getting a new job.

"I was going to ask you for a ride over there tonight, Zeb, but I guess you won't be coming." Cat held her mouth firm and crossed her arms over her chest.

"You're wrong about that, Cat, because I wouldn't miss this for the world. As soon as Thomas is done fixing the car, we'll go."

"All done," said Thomas, slamming the hood and wiping his hands on a rag.

"Good. Then let's get going. I have a job and I don't plan on being late." Cat headed out of the barn. Cappy stood up and swatted Zeb across the head.

"Ow, what was that for?" he asked, ducking away from her in order not to be swatted again.

"You're a nincompoop, that's why. You should have told her about the strippers." Cappy scowled at him.

"If you want to tell her, go ahead," Zeb said.

"That's not my position to tell her," said Cappy. "But if you know what's good for you, you'll stop all this nonsense and just accept Cat into your life and give up being a bachelor once and for all." She stormed out of the barn before Zeb could answer.

"Can I borrow something to wear?" Zeb asked Thomas.

"Are you really going to keep up this charade?" Thomas was the most sensible of all the brothers, and even a bit old-fashioned at times. He didn't have much of a sense of adventure.

"For now, I am. At least until after I take Cat to Burley's and she realizes the mistake she's made by taking that job."

"You're really not going to tell her about the strippers?"

"I won't have to. She'll figure it out once we walk in. Then I'll be there to save her and take her away. Don't worry, I won't let anything happen to her. I don't want to do this contest anymore, but it's going to have to be Cat's call to stop it. I'm not going to bow out of a challenge, just like you said. It's not in my vocabulary. Besides, I have a feeling that after tonight Cat will be the one coming to me and begging me to stop this whole thing, so it doesn't really matter."

"You'd better hope so," said Thomas in his all-knowing way. "Because if you keep walking around looking like that and driving cars like this, your bachelorhood is going to be over anyway. Then, after you and Cat break up, you're going to die as a lonely old man with regrets for not coming to terms with this whole thing while you had everything a man craves right in the palm of your hand."

* * *

BY THE TIME they finally arrived at Burley's, it was well past nine o'clock and Cat had told Burley she'd be there by eight to meet the girls and talk to them before they went on the stage.

It wasn't Cat's fault. Zeb took so long to pick out something to wear from Thomas' limited wardrobe that she thought they'd never leave. As it was, he ended up with a pair of jeans and a button-down checkered long-sleeved shirt. It was a working man's outfit, and nothing that Zeb would ever have chosen to wear if he didn't have to.

After that, Zeb played and fussed with his hair so long that Cat was starting to think they'd never leave.

"You don't have to be in such a foul mood," said Zeb, pulling up and parking in the lot.

It was crowded tonight for some reason, and Cat figured it was because Nate and his new band would be playing right after the girls did their routine.

"I'm just aggravated because you fussed with your appearance so long that we've probably missed the girls dancing. I told Burley I'd be here ahead of time and watch the show and tell him what I thought could be improved upon."

"Well, if you'd have let me use my gel, we could have been here an hour ago." He flipped down the visor and tried to see himself in the dirty mirror.

"You are incorrigible," she said, and opened the door to get out. She was wearing a plain button-down white blouse and a pair of jeans that were two sizes too big for her and without a belt. She had her hair up in a bun, not wanting to waste time by taking it down and having to brush out the tangles. She knew she looked horrible and probably smelled bad as well since Zeb wouldn't let her wear any of her perfumes.

Cat tired of this game and wanted to go back to the way things were, but she wasn't going to be the one to call it quits. If she did that, she'd be admitting that Zeb was right about her, and that was far from the truth. She'd also be more or less calling it quits to their marriage. While Zeb irked her at times, she wasn't ready to let go of him for good yet. He kind of grew on her with each passing day, and she started to like having him around. Oddly enough, even though they bickered it still felt right to her.

"Wait, Cat." Zeb reached out and grabbed her arm to keep her from going. Her eyes shot downward and her heart skipped a beat just by having his hand on her. She loved the feel of contact between them.

"What is it?" she asked.

"Honey, I really don't think you should go in there."

"I told you, you can't stop me. Now take your hand off of me."

"I can't let you do that. I need to tell you something first."

"Whatever it is can wait until later because I'm already very late. Now, please release me. If I'm not mistaken, the contract I signed said we couldn't kiss or hug and I'm sure this falls somewhere under your ridiculous bylaws."

"You did read the contract, and signed it anyway?" He let go of her arm. He seemed very surprised by the whole ordeal. Little did he know she was also a speed reader. Although she skimmed the contents of the contract quickly, she'd understood exactly everything she was agreeing to before she'd signed it.

"I'm not stupid, Zeb, no matter what you think." She made her way quickly to the front door. The heels she wore were old and hard to walk in, and she kept feeling the back strap slipping and was surprised she could keep them on at all.

"Wait up, sweetie. I don't think this is the type of place you should be walking into alone." Zeb ran up behind her and grabbed the door as she opened it, walking into the building in front of her, blocking her view. She heard some sexy music and also men whistling and shouting and wondered what was going on.

"Move over, Zeb, I can't see the stage."

"Exactly," she heard him mumble and didn't understand what he meant.

She pushed past him and stopped when her eyes focused on the dancers and, suddenly, she understood why everyone was acting so strangely toward her all night.

There were six female dancers, all topless with tiny little G-strings that covered a patch in front of their groins so small that she knew they had to have been shaved completely. One gyrated her hips at the end of the stage and a dozen hands reached up slipping money into her G-string. Two of the other female dancers embraced each other and actually made out, while one spun around the pole upside down with her legs spread wide and her boobs jiggling. The last one sat atop a patron on the stage doing a lap dance in front of everyone.

"Oh!" was all she could say.

"Now you see why I didn't want you to come here, Cat?"

"Couldn't you tell me this earlier?" she spat.

"I tried to tell you, sweetie. We all did, but you didn't give us a chance. Well, not really."

"I would think you would have tried a little harder." She turned to leave, but there were a few very large men coming in the door and, before she knew it, she was being pushed toward the stage.

"There you are, Cat," came the gruff voice of Burley. "Now get up there and show these girls how it's done, Vegas style, will you?"

"No, Mr. Burley there seems to be –"

It was too late. Burley shoved her up the stairs and onto the stage and before she knew it, she was standing next to a stripper with the lights shining directly at her.

"Cat, get down from there," she heard Zeb call out from somewhere in the room, but she couldn't see him. Then all the men started pushing forward and waving their hands at her.

"Take it off," yelled one of them, holding a dollar bill

toward her.

"Shake those tits," said another man who sounded drunk. Then one of the girls pushed her toward the men and their hands reached out for her.

"Get away," she said, picking up her foot to kick at them. When she did, the strap holding her shoe broke and the shoe went flying into the crowd.

That got more cheers from the men. One of the strippers reached over to unbutton Cat's shirt, and when she pushed the girl away, her shirt popped open exposing her bra. Cat jumped back, but the pants she wore were too big and slipped off and fell to the ground. Thank God, she wore panties today instead of her usual thong. It was only because of this stupid competition that she decided to change them.

"God damn it, Burley, get out of the way," she heard Zeb shout. Then she heard the sound of a fist smashing into flesh. The men in front of her continued to grab for her and she felt humiliated and ready to burst out crying.

"Come on, Cat, we're getting you the hell out of here," said Zeb, shooting up the stairs to the stage and putting his arm around her protectively. They were headed back down the stairs to leave when the crowd started shouting their disappointment. Suddenly, Cat felt Zeb release her, and turned to see all six of the strippers pulling him back on stage.

"Zeb, so good to see you again," said one of the girls, ripping his shirt right from his body.

"Ginger, not tonight," she heard Zeb say softly and wondered what that meant.

"Dance with us," said one of the other girls, grinding her hips up against him.

"Strip for us, baby, like you used to," came another plea from one of the strippers. Cat's mouth opened wide in surprise when she saw the girl starting to undo Zeb's pants right there in front of everyone.

"Licorice, Cinnamon, I said no. I'm a married man now," Zeb told them.

"Sure you are," said the first girl he'd called Ginger, reaching up and grabbing his face in her hands and licking his cheek and then plastering a big kiss on his mouth.

Cat had all she was going to take. She marched back up on the stage and ripped the girl named Ginger away from him and threw her off the stage into the crowd. The men went wild and started cheering. Coins hit the floor around her feet and dollar bills flew through the air when she pushed the other two away as well.

"No one is going to touch my husband, is that understood?" she ground out, looking over to the other two girls who just backed away.

"Cat, I can't believe this," said Zeb, looking at her with those sexy eyes and that half-grin that told her he wasn't being totally truthful. Another bill floated by in the air and Zeb reached out and snatched it up. "Holy crap, someone just threw a hundred dollar bill at us. That's the most I've ever gotten from . . ."

She knew he was going to say stripping, and she also knew if they didn't get out of there soon there was going to be a fight on their hands and it was going to get ugly. So she reached out and grabbed Zeb by the shoulders, loving the feel of his bare skin beneath her fingers. She pulled him forward and plastered the biggest kiss on his lips, and then backed away and saw the shit-eating grin on his face.

"You bastard!" she spat, and swung her fist next, hitting him right in the eye.

The crowd started getting way too rowdy, and the next thing she knew Nate was behind her, pulling her and Zeb off the stage.

"Here," he said, handing her the keys to Zeb's car. "The Mercedes is out back. You two get out of here fast before you cause any more trouble."

"I'm not finished," said Cat, but Zeb's grip on her arm said differently as he pulled the keys out of her hand and dragged her across the room.

"Thanks, Nate," she heard him call over his shoulder as they headed out the back door.

ZEB COULDN'T BELIEVE what had just happened. Nor could he believe the way his eye was smarting from Cat's punch.

"Get in," he said, opening the driver's door and pushing her inside. The top was down and Zeb realized Nate actually left his car open in a raunchy place like this. He was lucky the damned thing hadn't been rifled through or stolen by now.

"Taylor, get back here." It was the voice of Burley.

He heard the sound of sirens and saw Judas and his deputy's car come screeching up and stopping in front of the man. Judas jumped out and looked over at Zeb.

"Did Burley do that to you?" he asked, his left hand going for his gun since his right arm was still in a sling. His deputy jumped out with his gun already drawn.

"No, it wasn't him, Judas," cried Zeb. "Don't arrest him and, for God's sake, don't shoot him. It wasn't his fault."

"Then who gave you that shiner?" asked Judas, cocking his head and trying to get a better look at Zeb in the streetlight.

"It was me," came Cat's voice from inside the car.

"Cat? You did that to my brother?" Judas sounded impressed.

"She did and she's got one hell of an act," said Burley. "This is the biggest crowd I've had in months. They're all throwing money at the girls and it's not just dollar bills. Zeb, you and Cat come back inside. The crowd loves you two."

"Forget it," said Zeb. "Cat, move over." He got into the car quickly, almost sitting on Cat as she tried to make it over the center console of the small car. Then he put the keys in the ignition and tore out of the lot like a bat out of hell.

CHAPTER 13

Tarnished Saints

hey pulled up to Thomas' cabin and Zeb stopped the car. Cat hadn't said a word to him the entire ride but, then again, he hadn't said anything to her either. He put the electric top up on the convertible and then closed the windows and shut off the engine.

"Why are we stopping here?" she asked, finally breaking the silence.

"Because it's late, and I'm not going to go to the main house and be waking up Thomas' kids. Going back to my condo isn't an option either since Nate and his friends have taken it over."

He got out of the car and started for the door of the cabin and she ran after him. "So we're going to stay here instead?"

"For now. This is Thomas' cottage. He used to live here with the kids before he married Angel and moved to the big house." Zeb moved the rug away from the door and picked up a key hidden underneath and stuck it into the lock.

"We're breaking in?"

"Thomas leaves the key here in case any of us need to use the place." He opened the door and put the key back under the rug.

"We'll stay here tonight and in the morning, we'll figure out where we're going to live."

He walked in and turned on the light and Cat was taken aback by the small size of the place. "You said Thomas lived here? With all his kids?"

"Yeah, that's right. My brother lives simply." He turned and looked at her. "Not like us."

She realized his eye was swelled up and turning black and blue. "Oooo," she said, making a sucking noise with her mouth. "Sorry about that. Does it hurt?" She reached out to touch it and he jumped back.

"Yes, it hurts! Don't touch it."

"Quit being such a baby. I'll see if I can find some ice." She went to the kitchen and pulled open the freezer door and found a tray of ice cubes. She popped out a couple and wrapped them in a kitchen towel and turned around to see him lying on the sofa holding his hand over his eye.

"I don't get it," he said. "Why did you kiss me and then decide to punch me? You are a complicated woman, Catalina Cordovano."

"Yes, I am, and my name is Catalina Taylor, if I must remind you." She reached out and moved away his hand and put the ice on it, scooching up next to him on the sofa. "I kissed you for coming up to save me on that stage, and I punched you for knowing every one of those strippers by name."

"Oh, is that all?"

"Is that all? Here, hold your own ice." She went to get up, but Zeb pulled her back down and toward him, wrapping her in his arms and kissing her passionately on the mouth.

"Mmmmm, that's nice," she said, having missed this kind of attention from him.

"I'm sorry that I knew all those girls, but I'm a bachelor and a former stripper, so did you expect anything different from me?" He smiled that seductive smile that she knew he used on all the girls when he wanted them to forgive him. He was giving her those puppy dog eyes and she couldn't stay mad at him for long.

"No, I suppose not, you jerk," she said, sitting up and hitting him lightly on the arm. "But you didn't have to let me walk in there so blindly, did you?"

"I think you looked pretty damned sexy up on that stage," said Zeb, pulling her closer again.

"I was the only one fully clothed and you're saying I was the sexy one?"

"I guess I just kept picturing how you looked beneath those clothes. You know, sitting in a hot tub naked." His fingers wandered downward and before she knew it, he'd unbuttoned her shirt.

"You do realize that we're breaking the contract."

"You already did that the moment you kissed me up on that stage. Besides, I no longer care about the contract. I don't want to play this game anymore."

"Neither do I," she agreed, running her hand over his bare chest and down toward the buckle on his jeans. "So, who won?"

"Well, hopefully, we're both going to win by the end of the night," he said, slipping the shirt off her shoulders, leaving her in just her bra.

"No more wearing frumpy clothes?" she asked with hope in her voice.

"That's right, and no more driving a rusty old car," he added, expertly going for the clasp on her bra.

"Zebedee, you're being a bad boy," she said, playfully pushing away his hand.

"You are the one who said we're doing nothing wrong. After all, we're married."

"Hold it," she said, when he reached out for her again.

"Cat, please don't turn me away. I know I said we shouldn't make love, but I've changed my mind. I want to do it."

"Well . . . all right. Then give me a show." She got up off the couch and grabbed her blouse from the floor and held it in front of her.

"What?" he asked, sitting up and taking the ice and putting it on the floor next to his feet. "What are you saying you want me to do?"

"I want you to strip for me. The way you did for all those other girls when you put yourself through law school. I want you to seduce me."

"That's not seducing, that's teasing. I stripped but I never went further than a G-string, you've got to believe me."

"No, I don't. Nor do I care. Tonight, you're going to give me the show of a lifetime. Now, I'll be in the bedroom waiting."

Cat waited for a few minutes, wondering what was taking Zeb so long. Then, when she was just about to go find him, the door opened slowly and she heard music. His hand reach into the room placing a big boom box on the floor.

"Where'd you get that?" she asked with a laugh, since the music was not the normal music you'd expect for a stripper, but rather a scratchy Spanish radio station.

"I think one of Thomas' kids left it here," came his voice from behind the door. "Now, just be quiet because the show is going to start.

The light in the bedroom went off and Zeb's hand appeared inside the door again but this time he was holding a lit kerosene lantern. He put it down on the dresser, and appeared in the open doorway wearing what looked like a full zip-up mechanics uniform.

"Did someone call for an electrician?" he asked. "I hear the power is out?"

"Where did you find that getup?" she asked with a giggle.

"I think it's Thomas'," he said. "He keeps extra clothes here for when he's working on cars in the pole barn. Now quit asking so many questions, Cat. That's not what you're supposed to do at one of my shows."

"Well, sorry for never having seen a strip show before."

"Never?" He raised an eyebrow. "You worked in Vegas, sweetie, and you're telling me you never had the urge to check out what really happens there?"

"I wasn't interested in those kinds of things," she told him.

"Really?" he stepped closer, walking seductively over to the bed. "Well, I think you'll change your mind by the end of the night."

He did a few dance moves with his hands on his waist and gyrating his hips. Then he looked at her like he wanted to eat her and slowly undid the zipper to the one-piece jumpsuit. She saw he was wearing a sleeveless man's white undershirt and nothing else but his briefs as he stepped out of the suit and slinked his way toward her.

"Impressive," she said with a smile, feeling herself getting turned on by his actions.

"You haven't seen anything yet," he said, gripping the front of his t-shirt and ripping it right off his body. The sound of the tearing cloth filled the room and now he stood there in just his briefs that had a nice bulge to them.

"I don't think Thomas will appreciate you ripping his clothes," she said with a big smile.

"He's a man, he'll understand. Besides, you're the only one who needs to appreciate this. So are you?"

"I'm not sure yet. What else have you got?"

That question seemed to excite him and, before she knew it, he was flexing his muscles and she noticed his chest was glistening as he moved his torso in a way that reminded her of a belly dancer.

"Why is your chest so shiny?"

"Want to find out?" He moved closer, gyrating his pelvis right in front of her face. Taking her hands, he placed them on his chest. She used her fingers, sliding them down his chest and to his waist.

"Baby oil?" she asked, feeling her heart beating faster.

"Cooking oil," he said in a sultry voice. "It's because we're going to be cooking with fire tonight. Plus, it was all I could find."

"You are too funny, Zeb."

Next, he straddled her since she was sitting on the edge of the bed with her feet hanging over the side. He didn't sit on her lap, but pretended to do so, using great control to just tease her by touching her slightly with his bulge and then pulling away.

"I hope this isn't a normal part of your show with the ladies," she said, knowing that no woman could withstand the temptation.

"Only for you, Cat," he said, backing away slightly and turning around. He looked over his shoulder and then took a hold of his waistband, bending over in front of her and slowly peeling away his briefs until she was staring at his bare backside.

She licked her lips and waited anxiously for him to turn around. She felt herself dampening and starting to vibrate, and she could barely control herself waiting for what she'd wanted desperately since the day she woke up married to him.

"Turn around," she said, her voice barely above a whisper.

"Not so fast," he said, peeking at her over his shoulder with a smoldering look. "If I have to strip for you, then I want you to do the same for me."

"What?" That caught her by surprise. "Zeb, I don't know how to do that."

"I thought you were a showgirl at one time," he said.

"I was, but I quit when they wanted me to dance topless."

"Well, you know how to flirt, that's obvious. So, just take it a step further and seduce me."

"S – seduce you?" She didn't know if she could. Still, she was so hot for him at this moment that she would do whatever he wanted. She stood up and undid her pants and dropped them to the floor. "How's that?"

"Everyone in the bar saw that," he said without turning

around. "I want to see something that tells me you really want me."

"I do want you, Zeb."

"Then try it, Cat. Please?"

She didn't know if she could play this game. After all, wasn't it exactly what both of them were trying to stop doing? On the other hand, she didn't want to disappoint him, and she thought maybe it could be fun, after all.

She started gyrating her hips the way she saw him do. Then she took her hands and rubbed the oil from touching his chest earlier, onto her stomach.

"That's amazing," he said, sounding impressed. "You are a natural, honey."

"You do realize this is the only time I'm ever going to do this, no matter how much you beg me."

"Do what?" he asked, turning around slightly.

"My dance. My Seducing Zeb dance," she said, reaching back and unclasping her bra and holding it up in two fingers. He turned around fully at that, and her eyes devoured the biggest erection she'd ever seen. "Are you sure you never did anything like this at one of your wild bachelorette parties or whatever it was you used to strip for?"

"No, honey. None of them would ever be able to afford this kind of show. But for you – I'm going to give you the VIP treatment – for free." He flexed his other muscle then and she about jumped him she wanted him so badly. She wanted to also see him just as excited for her as she was for him.

So she turned around and looked over her shoulder and winked. Then she took a hold of her panties and slowly lowered them to the ground, bending over the bed as she did so.

That did it. He came up behind her and pushed his body against her, his hands fondling her breasts and rolling her nipples even though they didn't need any help being brought to peaks.

"Cat, I can't wait any longer. I'm going to burst right now if you keep teasing me like this."

"I'm not teasing," she said through ragged breathing as his hand slid down between her legs and he fingered her to make sure she was ready. She was more than ready. "I'm . . . just . . ." She could barely breathe. She felt so hot as his hands grabbed at her buttocks and he leaned forward, slowly lowering her toward the bed. "I'm just . . . Seducing Zeb," she said, then moaned in ecstasy at the feel of the tip of his manhood at her door.

"I can't wait any longer," his hot whisper said into her ear. Her legs went weak beneath her.

"Then don't," she said, giving him permission. She felt one slow thrust as he tested her to see if she could take in all of him. Then, when she moaned again, it must have pushed him over the edge because he pulled back and thrust his full length into her completely.

"Ohhhh, Zeb," she cried out as they continued to make love.

"Why did we wait?" he asked in a low, sexy voice. Suddenly, he pulled out, causing her alarm.

"What?" she turned around quickly. "You're not going to stop again," she said, more of a command than a question. If he walked away from her now like he did last time in the hot tub, she didn't know what she'd do.

"Are you sure we should do this?" he asked with a playful smile.

"Just try getting away and you'll find out the answer."

His eyes bored into hers, smoldering, turning her insides to fire. Then he slowly took a step backwards, and she knew he wanted her to come after him.

"You like the cat and mouse games?" she asked.

"Well, you are a Cat, aren't you?" He smiled and licked his lips.

"I'm a cat about to catch me a teasing rat." She ran to him and jumped into his arms, wrapping her legs around his waist. He entered her in this position, backing her against the wall.

129

"Cry out for me, Cat. I want to hear you release your sexual desires." One of his hands played with her breast as they continued to make love. She arched her back and cried out. It felt so good to throw caution to the wind and be free, finally.

Zeb carried her to the bed and they made love in so many positions that she lost count. He'd used ways of pleasuring a woman that she'd never even known. Each time he did, she had another orgasm. And just when she thought it would go on forever, he found his release, screaming out louder than she had.

Finally, they became still in each other's arms. Cat could hear the rapid beating of his heart as she rested her head on his chest.

"Would you say that counted as consummating the wedding?" she asked.

"Oh, I think that definitely counts," he said, kissing her atop the head. "Cat, there is no doubt any more that we are fully married and are now husband and wife."

CHAPTER 14

*C*at woke up early the next morning, having had the best night of her life. She looked over to Zeb sleeping next to her and thought how lucky she was to have someone like him after all.

They'd had a lot of fun last night. Although she didn't like the fact he'd been a stripper and done who-knows-what with any of the girls who'd been to one of his shows, she decided she wouldn't ask him any more about it. The less she knew, the less it would bother her, now that she was fully his wife.

She let Zeb sleep while she washed up and got dressed. Then she made her way outside to look around. The sun was coming up on the horizon and, in the distance, she saw the barn, a hen house, and a garden up high on the hill. She thought she heard voices and walked toward the hen house to find some of Thomas' kids collecting eggs.

"Well, good morning," said Cat to the boys. She remembered the older boy with the limp and that his name was Sam, but couldn't remember the youngest boy's name. He was the adorable one with the big green eyes and curly blond hair. "How are you doing, Sam and . . . Josh, is it?" she asked.

"My name's Eli," the little boy said, reaching his hand under a chicken and collecting an egg. The chicken cackled and tried to peck at his hand but he pulled it away quickly. "Josh and Jake are in the garden and Dan and Zeke are in the barn taking care of the horses."

"Oh, thank you for telling me that, Eli."

"Good morning, Catalina," said Sam with a genuine smile. The boy was starting to show some of that Taylor charm.

"Just call me Cat, Sam."

"Zeke has cats," Eli said, handing her an egg.

"Well," she said with a laugh. "Then maybe later, after school, he can show me. Why are you boys out here so early on a school day?"

"Pa makes us do our chores before we go to school," said Sam.

"He does, does he?" She wondered if Zeb would be such a strict father. Somehow, she didn't think so. Not after what she'd seen last night. She started visualizing their kids and wondering what they'd be like. Between Zeb and her, they were sure to have a wild side.

"Did you want some eggs for breakfast?" asked Sam. "We have plenty."

"Well, if you don't mind." She accepted the small basket of eggs that Sam handed her.

"You can have some vegetables, too," came a voice from behind her. She turned to see the twins standing there with their arms loaded down with vegetables from the garden.

"Why, thank you," she said, accepting a zucchini, a few small colored peppers, a small head of broccoli and an onion, as they loaded the vegetables into her arms. She didn't want to take too much, to make sure there was plenty left. After all, she knew they had a lot of mouths to feed at Thomas' house.

"Here are a few potatoes, some garlic and some herbs, too," said one of the twins, handing her yet another small basket.

"Oh, that's enough, but thank you," she said with a nod of her head.

"Hi, Cat!" said the eldest boy, Dan, walking out of the barn with the redheaded boy with the freckles named Zeke. Zeke cradled a cat in his arms.

"Hi, boys," she said, liking the way they all seemed to accept her though they barely knew her.

"There's not much in the fridge of the cabin," Sam told her. "But I think there's some cheese and some cooking oil in there."

"Yes, there's oil, thank you," she said, wondering if Zeb had used it all up on his body last night.

"There's pancake mix in there," said Dan. "We all love pancakes."

"Well, then maybe someday I'll have to make apple pancakes for all of you," she said. "For today, I think I'll make Zeb a breakfast skillet."

"Uncle Zeb likes vegetables," said one of the twins, she wasn't sure which. "He eats that tomato thing called Getta all the time."

"Getta?" she asked, with a chuckle.

"Josh, you idiot, it not Getta, it's called Bruschetta," said Zeke.

She could tell that a fight might break out over this, so she cleverly redirected their attention.

"Zeke, I hear you like cats. Is that one of your pets?" She reached out and ran her hand over the head of the tabby cat.

"This is Zebby," said Zeke. "I named him after Uncle Zeb. Zebby likes to chase mice."

"Oh, I bet he does," she said, feeling her cheeks flush at the thought of the little cat and mouse game she'd played with Zeb last night.

"Come on, guys, we've got to get back to the house so Angel and Gabby can cook up breakfast," said Dan. "They're waiting for us."

"Little Gabby cooks?" asked Cat, impressed with everything these kids could do.

"We all cook," said the other twin that she knew now was Jake.

"I don't want to make you late for school, so you'd better get along now," she told them. They all said goodbye to her and made their way to Dan's car.

After they left, she turned back to the house and felt a warmth inside her that had nothing to do with one of Zeb's sexual games. She felt the comfort of being part of a family. She loved all of Zeb's brothers and their wives and all the kids. They all seemed to like her as well. This felt right. This was where she belonged. Now that she and Zeb had made love, she was sure he would feel the same way, too.

There was no way he'd want to go through with the annulment now.

She headed up the stairs to the cabin to make breakfast for Zeb, feeling anxious. It seemed that every time something good happened in her life, it was followed by a huge disaster. Right now, she had that queasy feeling in her gut that maybe things weren't going to end the way she wanted them to, after all. God, she hoped she was wrong, because she didn't know what she'd do if Zeb decided that he still wanted to be a bachelor.

* * *

ZEB WOKE to the most wonderful aroma of fresh coffee and something cooking in the other room. He walked naked to the bathroom, then moved to the other room, coming up silently behind Cat as she bent over, peeking into the oven. She was wearing a cooking apron with flowers on it and had oven mitts on her hands. He loved how domestic she looked. He'd never seen this side of her before.

He pinched her bottom, making her jump. She turned around and hit him with her oven mitts.

"You scared me! Don't do that," she scolded.

Zeb laughed and took a step backwards. "Slow down, Slugger.

I already have one shiner. I don't need another one. It's not going to fare well with my new clients or when I show up in court."

"I'll put some makeup on it, and no one will be the wiser," she said, wrapping her arms around him. He took her in his arms and kissed her.

"I'm not sure about the makeup part," he said, kissing her again.

"Why not?" she asked, looking up into his eyes innocently. "I thought we were done with that silly contest. So now I can wear makeup again, right?"

"Yes, but even though you may be wearing makeup, I'm not going to be caught with that stuff on my face. I've got a reputation to uphold you realize."

"Hurry up and get in the shower," she told him. "I've got breakfast almost ready."

"I was hoping we'd have time for a little game of cat and mouse," he said, nibbling on her ear.

"Maybe tonight, in our new house," she told him. "For now, you'd better get some clothes on quick because Angel and Laney are coming over as soon as they get their kids off to school."

"What for?" he asked.

"We're going to look at the cabins today so we can pick out the one we're going to live in."

"About that," he said, scratching the back of his neck. "Maybe it's not such a good idea. I was thinking about the whole situation last night and I –"

"Oh, I'm burning my biscuits," cried Cat, hurrying over to the oven. "Now, hurry up and shower because I've invited the girls for breakfast and I think I see their car pulling up now."

Cat's biscuits weren't really burning. Just a few minutes ago, she'd popped them out of the can she'd found in the fridge and put them in the oven. She'd only told Zeb that in order to keep him from saying that he wanted to end the marriage, after all. She knew he was slated to be an eternal bachelor and she wasn't sure how he felt about staying married. Actually, she was afraid to bring up the subject to ask.

He'd hesitated when she'd told him they were going to pick out their lake house today, and that worried her. He wasn't thrilled with the idea. She needed to change his mind before he had too much time to think about it.

"Knock, knock," she heard Laney's voice at the door as the women peeked their heads inside.

"Is everyone decent?" asked Angel, looking around.

"Zeb's in the shower. Come on in," she told them, meeting them at the door. "Oh, you brought the baby!" Cat looked down to see the baby carrier in Laney's hand.

"Yes, it's my turn to watch little Matthias while J.D.'s at school," Laney explained.

"How is your daughter coping with being a mother at such a young age?" asked Cat.

"She's made a lot of changes in her life, but she really enjoys being a mother." Laney took the baby out of the carrier as she spoke.

"She sure has matured in the last month," said Angel, walking over and peering into the pan on the stove. "What are you making? It smells good."

"It's a veggie skillet," she told them, taking off the oven mitts and setting them on the kitchen table. "I'm hoping Zeb likes my cooking."

"Zeb's been a bachelor for so long that I'm sure he'll love anything that is home cooked," said Angel, walking over to sit on the couch.

"Well, I can't say the same for Judas." Laney tried to jostle the baby that was starting to fuss. "After all, the man still likes junk food over anything fresh."

"That'll change," said Angel. "Even Thomas has learned to cook, and the kids actually enjoy eating his concoctions now."

"Did you want to hold the baby?" asked Laney, holding him out to Cat.

Cat didn't know the first thing about babies and didn't really consider herself the mothering kind. She had no chance to say no as Laney pushed the baby into her arms. Little Matthias was crying but, as soon as Cat held him, his crying stopped.

"That's amazing," said Laney. "You stopped the baby from crying."

"I didn't do anything," she said, not even really sure she wasn't going to drop him.

"When are you and Zeb going to have one?" asked Angel.

"When are we going to have one what?" came Zeb's voice across the room as he came out of the bathroom with only a towel wrapped around his waist. The towel was a small one and Zeb had to hold it closed in front of him with one hand.

"We're talking about having babies," said Laney.

"Oh," said Zeb, once again not sounding too thrilled.

Cat wasn't sure she wanted to know the answer, so she figured she'd change the subject. "Honey, you might want to get dressed so we can eat."

Zeb walked up to her looking sexier than ever. Angel and Laney quickly looked in the opposite direction instead of at his bare chest.

"I don't have anything to wear that isn't ripped," he whispered into her ear.

She wasn't sure if the girls had heard him but, even if they hadn't, she was sure they noticed the reddening of her face as she started feeling very hot. Then she smelled the biscuits really burning this time and looked over to the stove knowing she had to remove them quickly.

"Here, hold the baby," she said, pushing Matthias into Zeb's hands and rushing across the room.

"Wait," said Zeb, reaching out to grab the baby with both hands as it started to cry again. She heard a gasp and then giggles

ELIZABETH ROSE

from Laney and Angel as she pulled the biscuits out of the oven just in the nick of time and set them atop the stove.

"Don't worry, everything's fine." She smiled and turned back to see Angel and Laney laughing and holding their hands in front of their eyes. Zeb had his back turned toward them, but she could see that he'd obviously had to drop his towel when she'd handed him the baby so quickly. He stood there stark naked and giving her a look that was somewhere between anger and amusement. The sight of him holding a baby so carefully that he'd not thought twice about dropping his towel to secure the child in a good hold made her realize that she was starting to love him. She wondered if she'd ever have the chance to see him holding their baby some day. Her heart said she would, but her head told her otherwise. This was all too good to be true and she was sure it wouldn't last.

CHAPTER 15

Zeb spent all morning returning his phone calls from his office, not able to believe how his business had grown since he'd opened up his own firm less than a month ago. He was already overworked, and felt bad for bailing out on Cat when it came to choosing a lake house, but he really didn't have the time.

Besides, he didn't care. He'd decided to stay in his condo though he hadn't had the heart to tell her yet. She seemed so excited to be choosing a lake house that he decided to just let her pick one out anyway. He told her he didn't care which one she chose, and that she could do whatever she wanted. He thought she'd be happy he was giving her free rein but she'd almost seemed upset by it.

It was probably a good thing to keep her busy since he'd made it clear she wasn't going to be going back to work for Burley after last night. He'd get his inheritance, although he really didn't care about it. He figured he could rent out the lake house to make some extra money.

Zeb rubbed his hands over his face wearily, still feeling the sting of Cat's punch. Damn, that girl was feisty. He never expected her to take on strippers or to punch him in the eye – and in front of everyone yet. She was jealous, and he liked that. He smiled and leaned back in his chair, thinking that maybe he could get used to this married stuff. He just needed a little more time to think about it.

Holding out his hand, he noticed the mark the wedding ring had left on his finger. It had been wedged on tight, but he'd finally managed to get it pried off his finger in the shower. It had been so tight, he felt as if it had been stopping his blood.

He wanted to talk to Cat about their relationship, but it just never seemed to happen. If they did stay married, he was going to buy her the best ring a girl ever had. It felt good to be back in his own clothes and driving his car again. Maybe Cat had been right about him using his money to get what he wanted, but he was used to this lifestyle and didn't want to change.

Thoughts filled his head about Cat making him breakfast and the way she looked holding that baby. Now, his head was all confused once again. He liked the way she'd looked at him when he was holding the baby, too. Of course, he was naked, so maybe that's what she'd been smiling about, he wasn't sure, but it almost felt – right. Zeb could almost picture himself being married to Cat the rest of his life. She was getting to him, and no woman had ever had that much control over him before. What was happening here?

He'd been thinking of making a phone call all day but was almost afraid to do it. But he knew now he had to try this, because maybe it would help to clear up some of the confusion in his mind. He pulled out his little black book with all his private numbers in it and dialed one in the back of the book that he'd just added this morning after some thorough research.

Hell, he hoped he was doing the right thing, because if he found the person he was looking for, life would never be the same for him or for Cat ever again.

Until he was sure of his whole situation, he could never let

Cat find out about this. Because if she did find out, he wasn't really sure how she would react. He gently touched his black eye with his fingers, and then picked up the receiver and punched in the number he'd written in black marker at the back of his book.

* * *

CAT CLEANED UP THE DISHES, still upset that Zeb wanted nothing to do with choosing a lake house. She'd relayed her concerns to Laney and Angel, but they didn't seem to agree with her.

"I'm sure Zeb is just too busy at work to have time to think about a house right now," said Laney, feeding the baby a bottle. "Judas gets wrapped up in his work a lot of times and he's hard to reach, as well."

"But Judas puts his family over his work," Cat pointed out. "After all, doesn't he take the baby to work with him sometimes?"

"Well, yes, but only because he has to."

"He doesn't have to. You could hire a babysitter but he wants to be around his new grandchild," said Cat. "Plus, he dove in front of a bullet to save his daughter."

"Thomas would give his life for any of our children as well," Angel said, drying the last dish and placing it back in the cabinet.

"That's different," said Laney. "Zeb doesn't have any kids, but he was a natural holding little Matthias, didn't you see that?"

"You . . . saw that?" asked Cat, feeling a little jealous.

"I didn't mean I saw his . . . I meant . . . help me out here, Angel."

Angel was laughing too hard to come to Laney's rescue.

"Well, maybe you two are right and I'm just paranoid that something is going to happen to ruin my happiness."

"You *are* paranoid," said Laney. "Just because things didn't work out for you in the past, doesn't mean that'll happen with Zeb."

"Every time something good happens to me, it seems it's

taken away by something bad," Cat told them. "Just like when my younger brother was born. I was so happy thinking we'd be like one of those real families, but then I lost him."

"It sounds like you had a real family," said Angel.

"No, I didn't. My parents never married. My father stole my brother, Lorenzo, from me and I never saw my brother again because he died. Then, when things started working out with my mother and we were almost able to survive on our own – she died, too."

"I'm so sorry," said Laney. "I guess I didn't realize that."

"I went from being a straight A student and homecoming queen to living like a bum out of a paper bag and sleeping in the gutters. Every time I heard the sound of a police siren, I ran, thinking they were going to put me in a foster home."

"I worked for Child Protective Services for years," Angel told her. "Plus, I grew up as an orphan so I know what it's like to live with foster families. It's not that bad. At least you would have had a sense of being part of a family."

"Well, I didn't know that at the time. I did have a family – sort of, when I turned eighteen and moved to Vegas. I was taken in by Cadmus Gianopoulos, the owner of the Diamond Dust Casino. That was after I stopped dancing as a showgirl."

Cat looked between the two women as she continued. "Cadmus and his wife, Sophia, took care of me and gave me a place to live. They also gave me a job in their casino, teaching me how to be a blackjack dealer."

"Wasn't that hard to learn?" asked Laney.

"No. It was easy for me because I was always good with math. I think they'd thought of me as the daughter they'd always wanted. Things were looking up until both of them ended up dying in a small, private plane crash. Once again, my good life turned sour. That's when their son, Denny, came into my life as the new owner of the casino."

"A boyfriend?" asked Laney.

"An abusive boyfriend who I'm glad to be away from."

"Oh, I can see why you're paranoid now," added Angel. "Don't worry, Cat, because the Taylor men aren't like that at all," she reassured her. "Just give Zeb some time and he'll come around. He's just used to living the life of a bachelor."

"He likes girls too much, too," Laney added, which didn't make Cat feel any better.

Angel gave Laney a scolding look at that comment and then forced a smile. "Cat, let's get going so you have time to see all the cabins and choose the right one for you and Zeb."

"All right. Just let me try to fix my hair," she said, going into the bathroom. "Hopefully, I can get a hold of my normal clothes again so I don't have to wear this ugly dress any longer." She looked into the mirror and started fixing her hair the best she could without having a brush, when she saw from the corner of her eye something glimmer. She glanced down to the top of the sink to see Zeb's wedding ring sitting there in a puddle of water. She lowered her hands slowly and picked up the ring and ran out to show Laney and Angel.

"What's that?" asked Laney, looking up from feeding the baby.

"It's Zeb's wedding ring," she said in a stiff voice.

"I'm sure he just forgot to put it back on after his shower," Angel told her.

"No, that's not true," she said with her heart beating faster. "He hasn't taken this off the whole time we've been married, even though I haven't been wearing mine. Now, we've finally consummated the marriage and he's taken it off. Don't you see what this means? He doesn't want to stay married, after all. I gave him sex and that's all he wanted. I've lost him, I know it. First, the way he didn't want to get a house and now this. Oh, girls, what am I going to do?"

"Do you love him?" asked Angel.

"Yes, I think I am falling in love with him," said Cat.

"Then tell him."

"No," said Laney. "The Taylor men don't do well with that kind of stuff."

"You're right," Angel agreed. "I remember how long it took for Thomas to say he loved me. We need to do something about this right away."

"Like what?" asked Cat.

"You need to seduce him," said Laney. "Make him want you as much as you want him."

"I've already done that, last night. It obviously didn't make a difference."

"Not sexually," said Laney. "Seduce him in other ways."

"Oh, I get it," said Angel. "Let him see what he'd be missing out on by not being married to you."

"I don't understand," said Cat, feeling very confused.

"Put it this way," said Laney. "Let him know the real you, not only the sexual side of you. Zeb is a bachelor. He's used to getting sex from girls."

"Laney!" Angel scolded.

"Sorry, Cat, I didn't mean it like that. I'm just saying, maybe he needs to see . . . what else you can do. What else you can offer and bring to the marriage."

"If you're saying be domestic, I don't think I can do that."

"You baked a wonderful breakfast skillet," said Angel.

"That's the only thing I really know how to make," Cat told them. "It was one of my mother's favorite dishes and we ate it several times a week."

"Cat, I'm sure you have a lot of talents Zeb hasn't seen yet," said Laney, putting the baby back into the carrier.

"Sure, if you're talking about dealing cards," Cat said, not at all sure she agreed with them.

"I have an idea," said Angel, getting to her feet. "Let's go find you a love nest and then you have some work to do to start changing Zeb's mind about not wanting to be married. You, my dear, need to start right away with learning how to seduce Zeb."

CHAPTER 16

*C*at spent a good part of the morning looking at the lake cabins, but none of them seemed exciting at all after having lived in Zeb's condo. She wished he was here to help her choose one, but she knew that was never going to happen. Finally, she decided on the lake house that had the most windows since Zeb made the comment how he liked to look at the lake because it calmed him.

"This one," said Cat, staring out the wall-to-wall windows on the front of the house that looked out over a hill and large lawn leading down to the lake. There was a pier and a small beach out front, and even a rowboat.

"Are you sure?" asked Angel, glancing at her watch. "After all, you've only changed your mind eight times since you've looked at them."

"I think so," she said looking over to Laney who still had the baby. "What do you think, Laney? Do you think Zeb will like it?"

"He'll love it," said Laney, picking up the carrier with the sleeping baby inside. "Angel, fast, give her the keys before she changes her mind. I've got to get back to the shop already. Nate was kind enough to watch it for me today, but I've really got to hire someone soon because this is just too much with having to take care of my grandson all day. I can't wait until J.D. graduates and can watch Matthias full time. I cherish these times spent with the baby, but I think I need a break."

"Good thing you don't have a baby of your own," said Cat. "If you did, you'd probably have to close your antique store."

Suddenly, Laney burst into tears and Angel ran over and put an arm around her.

"What did I say?" asked Cat innocently.

Laney and Angel looked at each other and then whispered something between them. "Go ahead and tell her," said Laney.

"Tell me what?" asked Cat, not understanding what was going on.

"Oh, Cat. Laney and I were going to keep our secret between just the girls for now," said Angel, not making any sense at all.

"What secret? What girls?"

"The secret between us – and also Candace. But now, since you're part of the family, we'll let you in on it as well."

"Oh, I love secrets," she said with a smile, happy that the girls were including her.

"I think I'm pregnant," said Laney with a half-smile.

"Really? Congratulations. So does your daughter or Judas know about this?"

"No," said Laney. "They've both been through so much lately that I didn't want to tell them until I was sure. But I am sure. I've been having morning sickness for the past week and I've also been tired and have skipped a period."

"She's not the only one," said Angel shyly.

"You, too?" asked Cat in surprise.

"Yes," Angel admitted. "Not to mention, Candace just discovered she is pregnant also."

"Oh, my goodness, there must be something in the water," said Cat with a giggle.

"That's right, so be sure not to drink it or you might end up pregnant as well," Angel said with a laugh.

"These Taylor men must be prolific at planting their seeds." Cat couldn't get over the fact that all three women were pregnant at the same time.

"Well, maybe not all of them," said Angel. "After all, none of the other nine brothers have kids. But then again, I'm sure they're being very careful."

"That's right," said Laney. "Zeb has a reputation for being with women. I'm sure he uses lots of protection."

"I . . . I'm not sure," said Cat.

"Didn't you two use protection?" asked Angel. "After all, I can't believe Zeb would be so careless if he's still planning on going through with the annulment."

"I guess we just got lost in the moment and the subject never came up. Besides," said Cat, trying to laugh it off, "we've only done it once."

"That's all it takes," Laney told her. "Look at my daughter. She did it once and now I'm a grandma."

"Or so she says it was only once," Angel pointed out.

"True," said Laney, looking down to the sleeping baby. "It looks like my baby and his Uncle Matthias will be growing up together. How odd is that?"

"I know exactly when I got pregnant," said Angel. "It was on our honeymoon in the Caribbean. It was so romantic. Thomas and I were excited not to have a bunch of kids around so we made up for lost time. I know Thomas will be thrilled when I tell him, because he wants twelve kids just like his parents. Still, I'm a little concerned because I've already got my hands full with seven kids already."

"Candace is so busy at the restaurant, and now I'm so busy trying to get my shop set up as well as take care of my new grandchild, that we are all exhausted," Laney added. "I don't know how we'll get through this."

"I can help," Cat volunteered. "I'll take that job at the antique shop, after all, Laney."

"You are a godsend, Cat."

"If Candace and Levi need any help with the books at the restaurant, I can handle all that for them, too. I love numbers, and when it comes to filing and organizing – no challenge is too big for me."

"Thanks, I'll tell Candace," said Laney. "She'll be elated since we all know Levi is no good with any kind of finances or paper-work. The past seven years will verify that."

They laughed and Cat knew they were talking about the fact Levi went to prison for not paying his taxes.

"Don't worry, I won't let that happen to him again, I promise," said Cat.

"You can hire yourself out as the town accountant," suggested Angel. "Almost everyone in town has their own business and no one likes to do the books. I'll let them all know at the next town meeting."

"Thanks, Angel." Cat was really starting to feel accepted and Sweetwater was starting to feel like home. It was a place where Cat could put down her roots and start a new life. She liked that. "Maybe I can help you out sometime, Angel, by watching your kids as well."

"That would be wonderful," said Angel. "The kids are at school all day, but since Thomas and Levi left this morning to pick up another car that Thomas is going to refurbish, I'm all alone. The men will be gone a few days and I planned on helping Candace at the restaurant. Dan and Sam are capable of watching all the kids, but I need an adult at the house with Eli after school and until I get back, in case CPS stops by on an unexpected visit. They'll stop coming by eventually, but it is still too early. It's just procedure."

Angel quickly filled in Cat on how she and Thomas met and everything they'd been through in the past few months. Cat realized that not only Thomas, but Levi and Judas as well, had all gone through some very trying times just like she had, but in a totally different way.

"I'll be looking forward to spending some time with the kids," said Cat.

"Then let's get back to the shop." Laney picked up the baby carrier and headed toward the door.

"I agree," said Angel. "Cat, the school bus will be dropping off the kids soon down at CR325. I'm sure Nate won't mind giving you a ride to where the bus stops. Then you can just walk back to my house with the kids and stay there until I'm done helping Candace at the restaurant if you don't mind. Oh, and Candace's twins and J.D. and the baby will be there, too."

"Sure," said Cat, wondering what she'd just gotten herself into. After all, she knew nothing about kids and, now, she'd just volunteered to watch nearly a dozen of them and all by herself. Well, if she could make it through this, then maybe if she and Zeb stayed married she would be able to handle having a child someday as well.

* * *

ZEB HAD WORKED late and it was already getting dark by the time he got back to Thunder Lake.

He was so tired from trying to juggle all his new clients and trying to find things in his messy office that he just wanted to have a cocktail and go to sleep. He still hadn't had the chance to organize his office, nor did he have a secretary. He contacted the employment agency and they said they'd send a girl over by the end of the week.

He pulled up to Thomas' house, somehow knowing Cat would be there. Sure enough, he could see her playing ball with the kids. She looked good in her tight jeans and t-shirt. Her hair was pulled back in a ponytail, and she wore a baseball cap on her head. She was up to bat. As he drove down the long driveway toward them, she hit the ball hard and it went flying right over his head. He was glad the top was down on his car or she would have hit it.

"Slow down, Slugger," he called out, knowing the power behind those beautiful arms of hers. His eye stung just thinking about it. It was starting to heal but he'd had a lot of people asking questions about it today. He'd had to lie and tell them he walked into a door in the dark because he wasn't about to tell him his new wife pasted him with a right hook.

He saw headlights in his rearview mirror and realized it was Angel's SUV with Candace's car right behind her. He wondered what was going on and why Cat was watching all the kids. He got out of the car and Cat came over to join him.

"Hi, Zeb," she said, pulling off her baseball cap and flashing him a smile. "How was work?"

"Grueling," he grunted. "I've got so much to do that I think I'm going to have to take on a partner. My office is so unorganized that I had to request a secretary today. Only thing is, she won't even be there until the end of the week."

"You don't need a secretary. I can help you with all that," she told him, but he didn't think it was a good idea for a husband and wife to work together. He knew that Levi and Candace worked together, but Levi was also not at the restaurant that often since his mayoral duties kept him busy at the town hall.

"No, Cat, it's fine. You just keep watching the kids." Her smile turned into a frown at his comment and he had the feeling he'd somehow insulted her. Before he could ask her about it, Candace and Angel walked up and intervened.

"Hi, kids!" Candace called out.

"Mom," shouted Candace's twins, running up to hug her.

"Now, Vance and Val, I hope you didn't give Cat any trouble." Candace bent down and scooped them up in a big hug and kissed them both.

"We didn't," Val said. "She's nice, we like her."

"Well, so do I," Candace told them.

"We brought some leftover food from the restaurant," said Angel. "Is anyone hungry?"

"Cat made us apple pancakes and peanut butter and jelly sandwiches," said Angel's daughter, Gabby. "But Josh and Jake had to show her how."

Zeb heard that and decided he'd better snag a sandwich or something from Angel. He was starving and wasn't sure Cat really knew how to cook even if she had pulled off an impressive skillet this morning.

"I'll take something," Zeb said, and Angel held out the bag and Zeb picked up a hero sandwich and a side of fries, popping a fry into his mouth. "Did you want one?" he asked, holding one out to Cat.

"No thanks," she said. "Not hungry."

"Okay, suit yourself. Oh, by the way, I told Nate he'd have to kick his friends out of the condo because we're going to be living there again. He said they'd be out by tomorrow."

"What?" She frowned and sounded so disappointed. "I thought we were going to live on the lake."

"Oh, that's right," he said. "About that – I'm not sure it's a good idea."

"I picked out a house for us to live in today. It's got wall-to-wall windows in the front," she blurted out.

"Honey, no place could have as many windows as my apartment. I don't plan on living in a small, musty cabin when I have a beautiful furnished condo right on the lake."

"The wrong lake," she mumbled, looking down to the ground.

"Well, you'll have to stay in your cabin for tonight," said Angel, interrupting. "So you two run along now so I can get the kids inside and ready for bed."

. . .

151

CAT KNEW Angel was trying to help her by sending her and Zeb to the cabin. She'd been so excited to stay there with Zeb, but now she was disappointed because it sounded as if he had no intention of ever living there with her.

She got in the car and they drove off. Once again, they were back to silence. The worst part was that Zeb didn't even seem to realize anything was wrong between them. He just kept eating his sandwich and turned the radio louder saying it was a song he liked. Cat felt like crying because all the happiness she'd found with Zeb last night was gone. Now, she realized she'd been happier before they'd actually consummated the marriage and became Mr. and Mrs. Zeb Taylor in every way.

at had faked being asleep last night when Zeb got out of the shower and came to bed, rubbing her back and obviously wanting sex. She was so angry with him that she decided she wasn't going to give him what he wanted until she got some kind of confirmation on his part about their marriage.

She rolled over in bed and the sun streaming in through the crack in the blinds hit her square in the face. She expected to see Zeb lying next to her and hoped they could talk before he took off for work. Instead, she found a note atop his pillow.

Pushing up in bed, she looked at the note and her heart fluttered. "Zeb?" she called out, but he didn't answer. She reached out with a shaking hand and picked it up, reading the words that no wife ever wants to hear.

"Cat, I had to go and didn't want to wake you since you were sleeping so soundly. I needed to leave early to stop by my condo for some things. I'll be out of town for a day or two, but I'll be back by the weekend. Have fun watching all the kids. – Zeb."

Her heart sank. As if it wasn't bad enough that he'd left without saying goodbye and didn't even tell her where he was going, he'd signed the note – Zeb. Not *love Zeb*, or *your husband, Zeb*, just . . . Zeb. She crunched up the piece of paper and threw it across the room, then slipped out of bed and made her way to the bathroom to brush her teeth. That's when she realized that she didn't even have a toothbrush with her. Yesterday had been so busy that she hadn't had time to go to the condo and bring any of their things back here yet.

She walked into the living room and glanced out the side window, never having taken the time to close the curtains properly last night. The window was dirty and a big splotch of bird poop left a blue and white streak right across the area at eye level.

She felt this was appropriate in her life right now. Wrapping her arms around her, she felt so alone at this very moment.

There was a knock at the front door and Cat ran over to open it, hoping it was Zeb coming back and knocking for some reason. She pulled open the door anxiously, hoping to see him.

"Zeb?" she cried out. But instead of her handsome husband, his plump, old aunt stood there with her carpetbag slung over her shoulder.

"Do I look like Zeb?" she retorted, pushing her way past Cat right into the house. "I came right over when I heard from Nate that Zeb packed a bag and left this morning."

Cat wondered how Cappy got here. She looked out to the driveway to see a red Chrysler convertible parked there. It looked like it was in prime condition although it was probably at least ten years old.

"Did you get a car?" Cat asked, and then remembered that Aunt Cappy didn't really drive. Only to drive-thru wedding chapels when she had to. She closed the door and followed the woman into the kitchen.

"I only drove from Thomas' house after Gus from the gas station dropped off the car I bought. I'm staying with Thomas for now since Nate has decided to let all those noisy band members take over the condo."

"Zeb said he kicked them out."

"He did, but I told Nate to stay there. After all, Zeb will be gone for a few days anyway. When he gets back, I'm going to have a talk with him about living in the lake house with you."

"Thank you for playing matchmaker, Aunt Cappy, but I really don't think you should get involved."

"Well, someone's got to do it or these boys will never get married! Why do you think I tried to match you and Zeb together from the beginning? You two belong together, that's why." She reached out and patted Cat on the shoulder.

"But – I was supposed to be marrying James, not Zeb, or did you forget?"

"I realize that, Catalina. I'm only glad I showed up when I did or you'd be married to the wrong brother right now." She put down her carpetbag on the kitchen counter.

"Are you trying to say that you knew all along I was marrying Zeb and not James but you didn't tell me?"

"Why do you think I convinced you to let me go get the marriage license for you? I didn't want you to look at his driver's license and realize he lived in Michigan and not Texas."

"Wait a minute. I was the one who asked you to do it. It was all my idea," said Cat, feeling confused.

"No, it wasn't. I just made you think it was." Cappy pulled open the fridge and looked inside, then slammed it shut, shaking her head and making a tsking noise with her mouth. "We'll need to go to the grocery store, too, I see."

"Aunt Cappy," said Cat, watching the old woman rifling through the cabinets next. "Why did you buy a car when you don't even drive?"

"I didn't buy it for me, dear," she said with a laugh, crossing her arms over her bosom. "I bought it for you!"

"For me?" Cat thought she'd heard her wrong at first. "Why would you buy me a car? You barely even know me."

"I bought it because you told me in Vegas that you didn't own a car and would love to have one some day. Besides, you're married to my nephew now and part of the family, so I can buy you gifts if I want to. If you're going to keep up with Zeb then you're going to need to be more independent and not have to rely on him for everything you need." She dug into her carpetbag and then held out a set of keys. "I figured this car matched your personality. It's fiery hot, yet with a convertible top to cool you off when you lose your temper. Just like Zeb. Besides, your husband can't have a convertible without you having one. It's not a new car, but it'll get by until Zeb decides to buy you what you truly deserve."

"Oh . . . I couldn't," she said, feeling very touched by the gift.

"Take it, and quit your babbling. We have a lot to do before Zeb gets back." She shoved the keys into her hand and Cat had no choice but to accept them.

"Why – thank you so much. No one's ever given me such a nice gift," she said, looking down at the keys that were on a keychain that looked like a little metal flower.

"Well, I don't know why they haven't. You are a beautiful woman and deserve to be treated better than that no-good nephew of mine is treating you."

"It's okay, Aunt Cappy. After all . . . we're not staying married."

"You most certainly are, if I have anything to say about it."

"What do you mean?" she looked up, surprised at the woman's bold answer.

"I see the way you look at Zeb. Plus, I know you like being married to him and also enjoy being part of the Taylor family, don't you?"

"Yes," she admitted, looking down and playing with the car keys. "I do. I feel like I finally have a place that I can call home. But I think I have more feelings for Zeb than he has for me."

"Nonsense. Men are just idiots and don't realize things because they don't like to get in touch with their feelings. They have some fool idea it'll make them weak or something."

"Do you really think that's it?" she asked hopefully.

"I know it is. Men are also stimulated by the senses. That, they respond to better than talking or trying to actually understand women."

"I know," she said with a smile, thinking about Zeb's striptease dance and also their passionate, physical night together.

"What do you want, Cat? Do you want to stay married to Zeb and live here at Thunder Lake? Or do you want to go back to Vegas and forget all about him?"

"No! I don't ever want to go back to my life in Vegas," she spat. "I want to stay here at Thunder Lake with Laney and Angel and the kids and everyone."

"I noticed you didn't mention Zeb."

"I was afraid to, Aunt Cappy. I want to stay married to Zeb more than anything but I'm afraid that every time I say aloud what's good in my life, something happens to take it away."

"It sounds to me like you need to attend one of Laney's meditation classes to clear your mind and get your wits about you again. Now, get dressed. She's having a class this morning and we're going to be there."

"Meditation class? What's that?"

Cappy didn't bother to answer. She just picked up her carpetbag and headed out the door.

* * *

ZEB SPENT all morning in court on another divorce case. He'd tried to postpone it, but he couldn't, after all. Although he'd won for his client, he almost hadn't because of showing up with a black eye. He had Cat to thank for that, but he really couldn't stay mad at her. He loved the fact Cat was a fighter and he wouldn't change that about her for the world.

He liked having someone who cared about him enough to get jealous, or to show him she didn't like his wild ways by punching him in the eye. It was like she left her mark on him, saying he was hers and she didn't want to share with anyone. He didn't understand it but, in some odd, twisted way, he really liked seeing this side of Cat.

Normally, being a bachelor, if a woman started acting possessive, he dumped her right away. But with Cat, her act of possessiveness made him want to keep her around instead. There was something deeper between them than he'd initially thought. He couldn't explain it, but the oddest thing was felt emotional about this and he was never one to waste time thinking about feelings.

Cat was right when she said they were both alike in their ways. And though it caused problems between them, it was also the common thread that bound them together.

She had a hard childhood and he admired her for her courage and everything she'd lived through and survived. After hearing her story, he started realizing that there was more to a relationship between two people than just sex and whatever money can buy. Maybe that was the definition of marriage.

He'd told Cat to look inside and, lately, he'd been looking inside himself as well. He wasn't sure about his insides, but hers were just as beautiful as her outer appearance. Zeb saw the way she'd looked so natural cooking in the cabin. When she'd held little Matthias, something stirred deep within him. Then when he'd held the baby, he'd almost felt as if it were theirs. He wondered what it would be like having a baby with Cat and which of them their child would look like.

While he hadn't realized it at first, Cat was as smart as she was pretty. Too bad he hadn't been giving her the credit she deserved. His wife was also creative and unique. He'd seen the way she'd been trying so hard to please him by getting jobs that he didn't even know she could do. He also noticed that his family and all the kids were accepting her wonderfully. Seeing her playing ball with the kids made him feel that she was already part of his family.

Doggone it, he liked having her around. She somehow fulfilled a part of him that had been empty for a long time now, but he couldn't quite explain it. Now, when he tried to picture his life as a bachelor and living without her, he was having a hard time doing it. Things and people were changing so quickly that it was making him question every little thing he did.

He walked out to his car with his brother, Nate, at his side.

"What's the matter, Zeb?" asked Nate. "You seem upset today."

"I guess all these divorce cases are just kind of getting to me."

"Oh, they're making you think of your annulment with Cat?"

"Yeah. I was so certain I wanted it but, lately, I've been thinking that maybe staying married to Cat wouldn't be that bad, after all."

"Your divorce cases made you realize this? I don't get it."

"Neither do I. Somehow, they made me realize that my relationship with Cat isn't as bad as I thought. We may not always agree on things, but I'm starting to think it doesn't really matter. Maybe we're both meant for each other, after all, like Aunt Cappy said. Oh, hell, I don't know." He threw his briefcase over the side of his open Mercedes convertible and got into the passenger seat. "Thanks for saying you'd take me to the airport," he told his brother.

"Not a problem," said Nate, getting into the driver's seat of the car and holding out his hand for the key.

Zeb reluctantly dropped the key into his palm. "No leaving the car with the top down and unlocked when you're doing a gig at Burley's," he told him. "Remember, you also promised to give Cat a ride anywhere she needs to go. And get your friends out of my condo because I'll be living there with Cat when I get back. Also, don't forget to pick me up at the airport and –"

"All right, already, Zeb," said Nate with a shake of the head. "You're starting to sound like a parent or something now that you've gotten married. What's happening to you? You also never told me where you're going."

"I'm going to St. Louis."

"Business?"

"No. And don't ask me anything else because I can't talk about it right now."

"All right, then let's go." Nate started the car and squealed out into traffic.

"Hey, Leadfoot, remember whose car you're driving here!"

"How could I forget?" mumbled Nate with a smile.

"As a matter of fact, maybe you should let Cat drive the Mercedes while I'm gone and you drive the old rust bucket instead."

"She won't need it now that she's got her own car," said Nate, changing lanes much too quickly.

"Her own car? Since when?" This was news to Zeb.

"I was over at Thomas' house earlier and Gus dropped it off. It's a fire engine red Chrysler convertible."

"What do you mean?" Zeb held on to the dashboard and grimaced at Nate's driving. "Did Cat have a car in Vegas and have it shipped out here? Or did she buy it in Michigan?"

"I heard she didn't have a car and that's why Aunt Cappy bought it for her. Gee, I wish she'd buy me a car, too." Nate reached over and clicked on the radio, but Zeb reached out and turned it off.

"Are you telling me Aunt Cappy bought Cat a car?" He wondered just what the old woman was up to. Somehow, he knew it had something to do with her controlling ways and matchmaking techniques, trying to get all the Taylor boys to do what she wanted and make them think it was their idea instead of hers. It was a game she'd always been very good at ever since Zeb and his brothers were just kids.

"Yep, she bought Cat a car." Nate found a pair of Zeb's sunglasses and slapped them on. "I sure could use a car, too. So if you're ever getting rid of this one, I've grown attached to it lately."

"Well, just get unattached because you're not getting it, and take off my sunglasses. Those cost more than any of your guitars. Nate, stop playing like you're so broke. I know you have enough money put away to buy your own car. Maybe not a Mercedes, but something halfway decent at least."

"I'm saving up for something important, like starting a business maybe. How do you know about that anyway?"

"I know because I accidentally opened your mail since you've taken it upon yourself to give the post office my address as your own."

"Well, I needed an address when I got back from the Caribbean and I haven't gotten a place of my own yet."

"Then rent a place of your own because you can't have mine," said Zeb, not liking the way Nate was becoming a little too comfortable in Zeb's surroundings lately.

"No, I don't want to waste money. I told you, I'm waiting for the perfect opportunity. I want to make a good investment and, at the same time, have my own business like you do, Zeb."

"I went to college and got a degree, little brother. It's something maybe you should have thought of years ago."

"We'll see," said Nate, smiling and nodding at a pretty girl as they passed a car. "I have an idea that might just take care of all of my problems."

"What's that? Marry a woman who can put your head on straight and keep your life in order?"

"Oh, you mean like you've already done with Cat?"

"Hah!" spat Zeb. "I might be married, but I've got my own life in order and I don't need a woman to do it for me."

"Really? Then why did Cat tell me when she came by to move not only her things but also yours to the cabin, that she was going to spend the next few days cleaning up your office and organizing it so you wouldn't have to hire a secretary?"

"She did what?" Zeb couldn't believe his ears.

"That's right," said Nate, heading toward the airport. "She said she was going to surprise you. I wasn't supposed to say anything but you're my brother so, of course, I had to tell you."

"What does she think she's doing by cleaning up my mess?"

"Well, isn't that what wives do?" asked Nate.

Zeb thought about it, and realized he was right. Maybe Cat was only acting like a wife and he should start acting like a husband. However, he wasn't sure he knew how to act that part.

They drove in silence while Zeb contemplated everything, until Nate finally spoke.

"So, you're staying married to Cat, aren't you?"

"We haven't really had the chance to discuss that yet."

"Have you done anything about stopping the annulment yet?" asked Nate, parking the car at the drop-off at the airport and pushing the button to pop open the trunk.

"Not yet. I've been too busy. If we do decide to stay married, I still have time to stop the annulment. I may have paid a little extra to rush the finalizing of it, but I know how slow the courts are, so I'm not worried." Zeb got out of the car and Nate followed suit.

"Who are you going to meet on this trip?"

"I'd rather not say."

Nate grabbed Zeb's carry-on bag from the trunk and handed it to him. "It's kind of sudden that you're leaving town, and you don't have much luggage."

"I'm only going to be gone for a day or two," said Zeb, taking his bag from his brother and slamming the trunk closed.

"What's this all about?" asked Nate, not letting up with his questions.

"Since I now know you can't keep a secret – it's none of your business." Zeb collected his briefcase from the back seat of the car.

"A little rendezvous?" Nate asked, raising a brow.

"I guess you could say that."

"I bet Cat would be surprised to hear about it."

"No! Whatever you do, don't mention anything to Cat, do you hear me? The last thing I want is for her to get wind of any of this." He headed into the airport, wondering if he was doing the right thing, after all.

CHAPTER 18

Cat sat with her eyes closed, breathing in the scent of sage incense and wildflower candles. She held on to an amethyst crystal, able to feel the vibrations running through her hands. The whole thing was totally amazing.

"Now, release your breath and slowly open your eyes," came Laney's soothing voice over the soft, relaxing music as she ended the guided meditation.

Cat's eyelids fluttered open slowly, and she looked around the attic room of Laney's antique shop. Aunt Cappy sat next to her on one of the large pillows on the ground, her lump of a body falling in between them. Cat wondered if they were going to have to pry her out with a crowbar.

"How does everyone feel?" asked Laney, turning on the lights and blowing out the candles. There were only two other people at the meditation. An older woman they'd introduced to her as the past mayor, Mabel Durnsby, and another woman a little younger than Mabel who was the wife of Gus who owned the gas station, joined them. Gus' wife was Pearl Kramer.

"This is always so invigorating," stated Mabel, getting up and brushing off her dress.

"Mrs. Durnsby, it's supposed to be relaxing, not invigorating," said Laney with a hand on her stomach.

"Come on, Pearl," said Mrs. Durnsby. "I'm having the school board over for tea this afternoon and we're using that nice antique dining room table that Judas and Laney gave me."

"Oh, do you mean that table that is the talk of the town?" asked Pearl.

"That's the one," said Mabel with a lusty look on her face.

"I think I'm going to be sick," said Laney, rushing from the room.

Mabel and Pearl said their goodbyes, and Cat walked downstairs with Aunt Cappy after helping her get off the pillows.

"I think that really helped," Cat told her new aunt. "I was able to see exactly what I want to do. It's all so clear to me now."

"Sorry about that," said Laney, coming out of the bathroom. "What are you saying, Cat?"

"I'm saying that I'm going to fix up the cabin on Thunder Lake so nice that Zeb won't care about living in his condo."

"Do you think that's possible?" asked Laney.

"Sure it is," Aunt Cappy broke in. "You have too much furniture around this place, Laney, so maybe you can let Cat decorate her place with some of it for now. It'll be a step up from that old lake house furniture that is worn and pretty sad looking."

"Well, I supposed that'd be fine," agreed Laney.

"I'll pay you for anything I take as soon as I start making money," Cat told her. "I have a little saved up from living in Vegas, but Denny's name is on the account, too, so I'm not even sure he hasn't cleaned it out by now. I have a few appointments to go over the books at the restaurant, the police station, and even the town hall, so that should help. Mr. Burley even asked me to come take another look at his books, too."

"Do you think it's a good idea to go back over to Burley's?" asked Laney. "Zeb won't like it."

"I don't care," said Cat. "I don't like the fact he went away for the weekend without telling me where or why and without even a kiss goodbye, but he did it anyway."

"That's men," said Laney. "Especially ones who have been bachelors too long. They think they don't have to report to anyone where they are or what they're doing."

"I wonder where Zeb went?" asked Aunt Cappy. "When I saw Nate this morning, he said Zeb only packed a carry-on and that he was going to be dropping him off at the airport."

"You don't think it's another woman, do you?" asked Laney.

Cat hadn't really thought about that. Now that Laney mentioned it, Zeb had seemed pretty secretive lately. "Laney, I know I said I'd help you out at the store today, but I'd really like to get over to Zeb's office and start organizing his desk if you don't mind." Now her motive of just helping him clean had changed. She figured while she was filing and organizing, she just might be able to find out what all his secrecy was about and maybe where he went.

"I'll help her here today," said Aunt Cappy. "You go on, Cat."

Laney covered her mouth and ran one more time for the bathroom, making Cat wonder if pregnancy was something she really wanted to experience, after all.

ZEB GLANCED at his watch once more and ordered another martini from the airport's V.I.P. lounge. His plane had landed an hour ago, and the man he was supposed to be meeting was late. The man's name was Lorenzo Rudawski, and he was a lawyer in St. Louis. He also could possibly be Cat's brother who she thought was dead.

Zeb had spoken to Lorenzo's secretary and made the appointment on the phone, but Zeb didn't tell him his true reason for wanting to meet with him yet. He'd done some research and found that Lorenzo was a good, fair lawyer and not corrupt as Cat had said her father had been.

Now, Zeb realized that Cat's father was even more devious than Cat had told him. There was no excuse for him to tell Cat and her mother that her brother was dead when he possibly wasn't.

"Excuse me, I'm supposed to meet a man named Zeb Taylor," he heard a voice from behind him and turned to see a tall, dark-haired man who had similar eyes and features of Cat talking to the bartender.

"I'm Zeb Taylor," he said, getting up and shaking the man's hand. "I take it you're Lorenzo Rudawski? I spoke with your secretary on the phone."

"I am," the man said, looking confused. "What can I do for you, Mr. Taylor?"

"I have a table reserved for us," Zeb said, motioning with his hand to the waiter. He slipped the waiter some money for holding the table and the man showed them to where they'd have lunch. "Please have a seat," Zeb told him. "I've got something to tell you that might come as a shock."

* * *

CAT SAT at Zeb's office desk piled so high with papers she could barely see over them. She was glad that Zeb had at least left a key with Angel and Thomas and that Angel had given it to her. If not, she wouldn't be able to clean and organize Zeb's office while he was away.

"This is unbelievable," she said, letting out a breath and swiveling around in the chair. The phone rang, and she stopped for a moment, not knowing where the sound was coming from. Finally, after digging through a pile of papers, she was able to find it and picked up the receiver and answered. "Zebedee Taylor's office, may I help you?" she spoke into the phone.

"Yes, I'm calling from the employment agency to let Mr. Taylor know we'll be able to send over a secretary this afternoon after all."

"Oh, that's not necessary," she told them.

"So, he's already found someone for the position then?"

"That's right, but thank you anyway."

She hung up the phone and looked around, figuring the best thing to do would be to organize some sort of filing system. She spied a file cabinet across the room and walked over to peer into it and almost laughed when she found it empty.

"Oh, Zeb," she said aloud. "You need more help than you think." She pulled a rubber band out of her pocket and pulled her hair back into a ponytail and rolled up her sleeves, ready to work.

* * *

"So that's the story," said Zeb, finishing off his bruschetta and pushing the plate to the side of the table. Immediately, the waiter was there taking it away.

"This is amazing and unbelievable," said Lorenzo with glassy eyes. "I truly thought Cat as well as our mother had died years ago. That's what my father led me to believe. I never thought to investigate it for myself."

"It seems that is what he told them about you, too. I assure you, Cat is alive and well and I think she would love to see you again."

"I'd love to see my sister," said Lorenzo, nodding to the waiter as he placed their lunch in front of them. "Tell me, how did you meet Cat in the first place?"

"That's a funny story," he said, looking up at the waiter. "Please bring us another round of drinks and make sure I get the check."

"So you and Cat are married?" he asked, trying to understand.

"Uh . . . yes. We are married."

"Well, congrats," said Lorenzo. "How many nephews and nieces do I have?"

"No," Zeb said with a wave of his hand. "No kids. We just got married."

"Well, knowing Cat, she'll have your whole life planned by the time you get back."

"What?" He didn't want to hear this.

"My sister is great with organizing and likes to be the one in charge. It's hard to tell her no. I know because she never let me get away with anything when we were growing up."

"Are you about the same age?" Zeb asked him.

"Cat is a few years older than me. I was only ten when my father left and took me with him. He wanted a son who would be just like him. That's why he put me through law school. Did your father do the same for you?"

"No," said Zeb, nodding thanks to the waiter as he put down their drinks. Zeb waited until the man left the table before he continued talking. "My father was a preacher and I come from a family of twelve boys. He didn't have money for any of us to go to college."

"How did you pay for law school then?" Lorenzo picked up his drink.

"Let's just say I had to take on a night job."

"You know, Cat always wanted to be a professional someday. She had high hopes to be very successful and, of course, rich, once she finished high school. Did it ever happen?"

Zeb looked at Lorenzo who seemed so well-off and very successful. Then he thought of Cat and her sad story of what she'd gone through growing up. It didn't seem fair. Cat had to give up her dreams and Lorenzo had everything, all because of a crooked lawyer father. Suddenly, he wondered if Cat was going to resent her brother because of this.

"No, Cat never had the chance to finish high school," he told Lorenzo.

"That's too bad. I'd like to help her out financially any way I can," he offered.

"You would?" he asked, thinking this didn't sound at all like something Cat's father would have done and that it was a good indication that Zeb's gut feeling about Lorenzo being a good guy was correct, after all.

"I'll do what I can," he told him. "But I have to tell you the truth that since I've opened my own law firm, it hasn't been going that well. I've been thinking of finding a partner and moving. The problem is that my wife and daughter like it here, so it'll take some convincing. Especially since my wife is due to have another baby any day now."

"You're married and have a family?" asked Zeb.

"I am. I'd love for them to meet you since we're brothers-in-law now. Why don't you stay the night with us? That is, unless you've already made other plans."

Zeb thought about it for a moment. He didn't know these people at all, but he already liked Lorenzo. He would love to meet his family and maybe find out more about Cat while he was at it.

"Thank you, that'd be great," he said.

"All right then, I'll call my wife and let her know right now." The man picked up his phone and then looked at Zeb. "Didn't you want to phone Cat and tell her anything?"

"I thought I'd surprise her and was hoping I could get you to show up without her knowing you're coming."

"Oh." He nodded his head. "All right. I can do that. I can't wait to see Cat again after all these years."

"I'm sure she'll be just as excited." Zeb suddenly realized that he didn't know if this was true. Cat said she'd had a close relationship with her brother, but maybe he should have spoken to her about this first. Then again, he thought, picking up his fork, Cat always said she liked surprises. Well, he planned on surprising her more than she'd ever been in her life.

at had never felt more wanted or needed in her entire life. She'd spent the last two days going over the books for the diner, the police station, and even Burley's bar. She had more requests for her services than she'd expected.

Everyone ended up paying her twice the amount she'd quoted them, saying she was underselling herself. All but Burley, who gave her an I.O.U. because he was so broke that she actually felt sorry for him.

Judas had finally done something about the strippers in the bar and put out an ordinance saying stripping wasn't allowed in Sweetwater anymore. The girls left, and with them went all Burley's regular customers. He'd put a *for sale* sign out front last night and she knew whoever bought the place was going to get it for a steal.

She sat at Zeb's desk, yawning since it was late in the day and she realized she hadn't even had the chance to eat today. She was only glad that Thomas and Levi were back from their trip because now they were able to help out with things and that would take pressure off of all the pregnant women.

Judas had already guessed that Laney was pregnant and he

was elated as well as horrified at the same time not knowing what to do to be a father. Their daughter, J.D., said as soon as she graduated high school she'd be free to help her mom with the new baby as well as take care of Matthias. According to Laney, her daughter had changed so much that she also wanted to start doing day care.

Cat was in a hurry to finish organizing Zeb's office because she'd been invited to stop by Angel's house later. Tonight, Angel and Candace were going to make the announcement to everyone that they were pregnant. She couldn't wait to join in the celebration.

She was almost ready to leave when the door to the office opened and two young women dressed much too sexy for being clients walked in.

"Is Zeb here?" asked the one with the big boobs and the brown hair.

"I'm sorry, but he's out of town," said Cat. "If you want to make an appointment, you'll have to come back next week."

"He's already rescheduled our appointment. We are supposed to go out," whined the shorter one with the tattoos and the blond hair.

"Go out?" Cat's head snapped up and she realized these women weren't clients. They were dates.

"Yes, he's supposed to show us his condo," said the brunette.

"He's also going to show us his king-sized bed," added the other one with a giggle.

Cat's jaw dropped open not able to believe what she was hearing.

"Are you the secretary?" the first girl asked.

"No, I'm not the secretary," she said with a stiff upper lip. "I am his wife!"

"What?" asked the blond one. "Zeb never told us he was married."

"Well, it all came on suddenly," she answered.

"Suddenly? But we saw Zeb a few days ago and that's when he postponed our date," said the dark-haired one.

"No," said Cat, shaking her head, not wanting to believe it. "I'm sure you're mistaken."

"Not as mistaken as you are about your husband," the girl answered. "Don't you know you can't trust lawyers?"

"Get out!" Cat shouted, standing up quickly and pointing to the door. If the girls stayed another minute, she was going to walk over and throw them out herself.

"Take it easy, we're going," they both mumbled and left right away.

Cat slumped back down atop the chair and felt like she was going to cry. She opened the desk drawer to look for a tissue and instead found a little black book. She reached out to pick it up, her hand shaking slightly since she knew exactly what it was.

Sure enough, she flipped through it and found one girl's name and number after another, and not a single male name inside. To top it off, he'd even rated the girls with one to five stars.

"You pig!" she said, throwing the book into the garbage. When she did, a page fluttered out and fell to the ground. She picked it up and looked at it, realizing it was the number of an airline flight with yesterday's date on it. There was also a phone number after it written in big, bold, black marker. She was going to throw it out as well, then wondered if this is where he'd gone. She had to know if he was with another woman and decided she was going to call the number on the paper.

Cat picked up the desk phone but then realized if it was a woman's cell phone and she saw Zeb's office number on it, she'd tell him and he'd know she was spying on him. Instead, she picked up her own cell phone, hoping whoever answered wouldn't recognize the number and she could claim she'd misdialed.

She punched in the number and it rang twice. Cat's heart about beat from her chest as she waited for someone to answer.

"Please be a male, please be a male," she muttered, listening to it ring for the third time. Then someone picked up and said hello and to her disappointment, it was a woman's voice. She quickly clicked off her phone without saying a word, feeling that their marriage was truly over.

The office door opened and the mailman came in and handed her Zeb's mail and then turned around and left.

She put the bills on the desk, noticing a letter peeking out that looked different from the rest. She picked it up and noticed it was from the court in Vegas. Tearing it open, she nervously scanned the paper inside. It was the Decree of Annulment signed by the judge. If she understood it correctly, it said there was no need for a court date since they'd both signed the papers and agreed. In other words, their annulment was now finalized. Cat felt faint and tears filled her eyes. She and Zeb were no longer married.

CHAPTER 20

Zeb was sitting in Lorenzo's kitchen playing checkers with the man's three-year-old daughter, Alissa, and eating ice cream when the phone rang. Lorenzo's pregnant wife, Maria, went over to answer it.

Zeb purposely lost the game and acted surprised as Alissa jumped his last checker on the board.

"Oh, you win!" he said shaking his head. "I can't beat you. You are too good at this game."

The little girl laughed. She looked so much like Cat when she smiled, that Zeb started realizing how much he missed his wife. He felt at home with Lorenzo and his family. They'd asked him to stay for two nights, and Zeb had agreed to take them up on the offer.

He could see himself being married and having a family now with Cat. Hopefully, someday, they'd even have a child of their own. It was clear to him now that he'd been holding on to bachelorhood so hard that if he didn't let go he was going to lose the best woman who'd ever come into his life.

"Who was on the phone?" Lorenzo asked his wife.

"I don't know, they hung up on me," she answered. "Honey, I

didn't realize until after I answered that it was the line from your office that transfers over here when you're at home. I guess it was a wrong number. The caller ID said Cordovano. Why does that name sound familiar? Wasn't that your mother's maiden name?"

Zeb and Lorenzo both looked at each other.

"That's my wife and your husband's sister," announced Zeb. "It's Cat, I'm sure of it."

Lorenzo's wife took their daughter and headed upstairs.

"Do you think that was really my sister calling?" asked Lorenzo.

"Only one way to find out." Zeb went over to their phone and hit the redial button.

"Hello?" came Cat's voice from the other end.

"Cat?" asked Zeb. "Did you just . . . call here?"

Silence came from the other end of the phone.

"Where are you, Zeb?"

"I'm in St. Louis," he said, not lying. "How did you get this number?"

"Does it really matter?"

"Honey, you sound angry about something."

"Why haven't you called me since you've been gone?"

He realized now that maybe he should have called, but he'd been on his own so long that he wasn't used to telling anyone where he was or what he was doing or when he was coming home.

"Is everything all right, Cat?"

"You had a couple of visitors at the office today," she said snidely. "They wanted to see your bedroom and try out your king-sized bed. They said you postponed their date."

Zeb cringed, knowing exactly who she was talking about. He also knew now that he'd made a huge mistake when he saw those girls and tried to avoid them without telling them he was married. He was not really going to date them while he was married to Cat, but he just couldn't bring himself to say the M word in front of girls at the time.

"Cat, I can explain all that."

"The mail came today and there's a certain piece you might be interested in."

"Just leave the mail on my desk."

"Are you going to tell me who you're with or not?"

"I . . . can't," he said, looking at Lorenzo, not wanting to relay information as important as this over the phone. "You'll find out as soon as I get home. I guarantee when you find out who I've been with and what I've been doing, your life will never be the same again."

He heard a click on the other end and realized she'd hung up on him. He looked at the phone and then redialed. Her phone rang several times but she didn't pick up. Then it finally went to voice mail. He listened to the automated voice on the other end that sounded like a male robot. It only made him desire to hear Cat's voice more than ever now.

"Honey, don't be mad at me," he said into the receiver as he left a recorded message. He thought about the fact that Lorenzo had asked if he was going to call her earlier and he hadn't done it. He also thought about Jenny and Melody and how he should have shook them off and told them the truth inside of avoiding the issue. Now he wished he had. "I've been a bachelor for a long time, and sometimes I just can't change my ways. Please, just accept me for who I am. I'll be home tomorrow and I'm bringing someone home with me. I've got something important to tell you. This is going to change both of our lives forever, Cat. It's already changed mine more than you can imagine. Okay, I'll see you soon. Bye."

* * *

CAT LISTENED to the message Zeb left her, not able to believe he was breaking up with her over the phone and on voice mail yet. She'd given him the opportunity to tell her he was with another woman, but he didn't do it. She'd also given him the chance to say he was sorry for trying to make dates with floozies when he was married to her, but instead he told her he was a bachelor so long that sometimes he couldn't change his ways. He even had the nerve to say she should accept him. Hah! Like that was ever going to happen.

She left his office and made her way to her car, not knowing where to go now. She wanted to go to Angel but that would only make her feel more miserable when they were all celebrating the new pregnancies. Besides, she didn't want to ruin their happy moment by telling them the news that she and Zeb were no longer married and he was bringing home another woman.

Cat found herself driving aimlessly in the dark. Before she knew it, she spotted the light-up sign atop Burley's Bar and pulled into the lot. Isn't this where single people down on their luck usually went? Maybe she'd just spend a few hours here drinking wine before she went back to her empty cottage and spend the night sleeping alone while Zeb was sharing a bed with another woman.

She went into the bar and sat at the counter, wondering what was taking Burley so long to wait on her. There seemed to be a buzz amongst the customers tonight so she stopped a man walking past to ask him what everyone was talking about.

"Didn't you hear?" the man asked. "Burley's gone. Some guy from out of town is going to buy the place and he's already here right now."

"Really? Who?" she asked.

"Not sure what his name is, but I think he's from Vegas."

"Vegas?" The blood froze in her veins. She had a feeling this was not good. Then when the bartender walked up and placed a glass of white wine in front of her before she'd even ordered, she got a sick feeling in the pit of her stomach.

"White wine for my best blackjack dealer," the man said. Her eyes snapped up to see Denny Gianopoulos standing in front of her.

"Denny!" she said, quickly vacating the stool. "What are you doing here?"

"Looking for you, sweetheart."

"How did you find me?"

"I had the tracking device on your phone activated years ago. Why do you think I bought you a phone to begin with?"

The slimeball. It was just like something he'd do. "What do you want?" she asked guardedly.

"I'm buying the bar, Cat. I even managed to get the strippers back. Care to dance again?"

"You know I never stripped and that I'd never do that so don't bother asking."

"I also found out that gambling is now legal in Sweetwater and the surrounding towns. I plan on turning this bar into a casino. We're starting the gambling tonight and you, my dear, are going to deal." He grabbed her wine in one hand and walked around the bar and dragged her to a table he'd set up as a black-jack table. "Gather round everyone, as we have here a professional blackjack dealer straight from Vegas. The game is starting now so put down your money and phone your friends to join us."

"Denny, I don't work for you anymore," she spat.

"You're still mine, Cat, and I plan on marrying you, even if I no longer own the Diamond Dust Casino thanks to your pretend husband exposing my employees cheating. I don't care. I've managed to keep from being arrested and we're going to start fresh right here in good ol' Sweetwater."

"You bastard! Let go of me before my husband has your head."

"Stop the act, Cat. I know you're no longer married. You're friend, Bill, at the County Clerk's Office in Vegas told me they mailed you your finalization for your annulment days ago. I also know that Zeb Taylor is out of town and can't come to your rescue, nor would he, since he's got a reputation for not being a one woman man. Now, sit down and deal."

Cat saw a lot of Denny's goons standing around the table and not a single soul that she knew. She wouldn't be able to just walk out of here without them stopping her. So, she did the only thing she could. She sat down and dealt the cards, but there was no way in hell she was going to help Denny cheat the people ever again.

* * *

ZEB WAS on the phone for an hour trying to get an earlier flight back home, but everything was booked solid. He had an awful feeling that he screwed things up royally between him and Cat and just wanted to be able to hold her and tell her he was sorry. Maybe he should have just told her about her brother, he realized, but she wouldn't answer her phone. Her voice mailbox was full so he couldn't even leave a message. This was something he needed to tell her himself, or he would have just asked one of his brothers to relay the message for him.

"Is something the matter?" Lorenzo asked, sitting down across from him at the table.

"I don't know," he said, clicking off the phone. "Cat seemed pretty mad at me. I should have just told her about you."

"I'd hate to see things go bad between you two."

"I need to get home, Lorenzo. I've decided I'm going to ask your sister to marry me."

"I thought you said you were already married."

"I'm going to do it the right way this time. If Cat will stay married to me, I'm going to give her the biggest, classiest wedding and buy her the fanciest ring ever."

"Do you think she'd like that?" asked Lorenzo.

Zeb suddenly wondered if she would. Or would she say he was only using his money to try to buy her? After all, that was what she'd accused him of doing with everything else.

"I'm not sure anymore," Zeb admitted. "All I know is that I want to spend the rest of my life with Cat."

"Then tell her," Lorenzo urged him. "I've got to warn you, though. Knowing my sister, she tends to hold a grudge. Even when you say you're sorry, she somehow never believes it."

"Then I'll just have to show her," Zeb said. "To do that, I think we should start with you."

"What do you mean?" asked Lorenzo.

"You said you wanted to work with another law firm rather than to be on your own. Well, I'm looking for another lawyer to work with me because I'm swamped and could use help. Why don't you and your family move to Michigan and you can work for me? That way, you will be closer to your sister. If everything goes well and we both like it, I might even take you on as a partner."

"Really? I'd love that, Zeb. I think Maria would go for it, too. You've got yourself a deal." They clasped hands and shook.

"I've got to get back to Sweetwater right away. Can you give me a ride to the airport? I'm going to fly stand-by. It would be good if you came, too. Maybe then Cat will see what I've been doing and believe me."

"Of course. I'll pack a quick bag and let's go."

They were at the airport half an hour later when Zeb's phone rang and he picked it up to hear his brother, Nate, on the other end. There was loud music in the background and lots of talking. It sounded like Nate was probably getting ready for a gig at Burley's.

"Nate, I can hardly hear you," said Zeb. "What's up?"

"It's Cat," he heard his brother say. "She's here and she's dealing blackjack."

"What?" asked Zeb, thinking he heard him wrong. "Did you say Cat is dealing blackjack?"

"It's that new owner. I think he talked her into doing it. She doesn't look happy."

"What new owner?" he asked. "And why the hell aren't you doing something about it?"

"What did you say, Zeb? I can't hear you. This Denny guy is a real ass. He's playing the music so loud and I'm not even sure the band is going to get a chance to perform."

"Denny?" Zeb asked. "Did you say Denny?" There was a lot of static over the phone and they started breaking up.

"Can't hear you, Zeb. If you can hear me, you may want to get home quickly. I don't like this guy and I think he's got the hots for Cat. Okay, gotta go." The phone clicked off.

Zeb stood there in shock, staring into space. What would Denny Gianopoulos be doing in Sweetwater? Did Nate say the creep now owned Burley's. He hoped not. He also hoped that Cat hadn't gotten back together with him because that would be the last thing he'd want to hear.

"Zeb," said Lorenzo. "They say they have only one seat open on stand-by. You take it and I'll phone you when I catch a plane."

"Thanks, Lorenzo," said Zeb, heading down the ramp to the plane and at the same time dialing his brother's number.

CHAPTER 21

Cat was still dealing blackjack three and a half hours and five glasses of wine later, with Denny watching over her like a hawk. She saw Nate and the band looking over at her while they played but she couldn't even signal to him that something was wrong.

She finished the hand and Denny bent over and whispered in her ear. "You're not doing your job, honey. Some of these men are winning too much. Now work your magic and get it back fast," he said, sliding his hand onto her lap and giving her knee a tight squeeze. She reached down and shoved his hand off of her.

Cat picked up the discarded cards and was about to use her sleight of hand routine, then realized that she couldn't live this way any longer. "No! I won't do it," she said, and threw the cards into the air and stood up.

"What the hell do you think you're doing?" Denny growled.

"I'm not working for you anymore, and I'm surely never going to marry you, Denny. I want nothing to do with you ever again."

His men started circling around her like a pack of wolves. Cat never felt so alone as right now. The band stopped playing and she saw Nate whisper something to the other band members. She tried to leave the table but when she did, Denny's hand snaked out and gripped her wrist tightly.

"Get your filthy hands off my wife!" she heard, and looked up to see Zeb pushing through the crowd and jumping through the air, knocking Denny to the ground.

"Zeb!" she shouted, moving out of the way, watching as the two men threw punches and rolled around the ground. Then two of Denny's men pulled Zeb off of their boss and held him while Denny punched Zeb first in the gut and then in the face. Denny was left-handed and that meant Zeb took a punch to his good eye, leaving him now with two black eyes instead of one.

"No!" she cried, trying to run to Zeb, but another of Denny's goons held her back.

"No one is going to hurt our brother," came a shout from across the room. Before she knew what was happening, Levi and Thomas shot through the crowd, pulled the men off Zeb, and started fighting as well.

Cat was still helpless, being held back by one of Denny's men though she struggled to get out of his hold.

"Your husband has a lot of brothers," said the man.

"More than you think," came another voice. This time, Nate walked up and punched the man holding her, causing him to release her. Then the band members got into the fight and the whole bar was up in arms.

"Are you all right, Cat?" asked Zeb, running over to her.

"I'm fine," she said. "Watch out!"

Zeb turned just in time to block a punch and then continued fighting.

"The cops are here. Run!" she heard one of Denny's men call out. That's when she heard the sirens and saw Judas and his deputy run in with their guns drawn.

"All right, everyone stop!" shouted Judas, holding his gun in his left hand since his right arm was still in a sling.

"Like you're going to stop us," said one of the men sarcastically, reaching for the money on the table.

Judas fired a shot in the ceiling just above the man's head. A large piece of plaster fell and knocked him out.

Then, with the help of Zeb and his brothers, Denny and his men were all rounded up and cuffed and hauled out of the bar.

"Cat, come here," said Zeb, putting his arms around her.

Cat leaned against Zeb's chest and started crying. Everything in her life had been going so good and, now, everything had seemed to turn sour once again.

"Come on, I'm taking you back to the condo," he said.

"No." She stepped away and held out her hand. "I'm not going to sleep in that bed knowing how many other women have slept in it with you."

"Fine, then we'll go back to the cabin instead. But let's just get the hell out of here."

* * *

WHEN THEY GOT BACK to the cottage and went inside, Cat was feeling sick. Her head spun from drinking too much wine and she was nauseated from the smell of all the cigar and cigarette smoke in the bar. She didn't miss her life working in a casino in Vegas and, after tonight, she never wanted to see a casino or a pack of cards again.

"Cat, we need to talk," said Zeb, sitting down on the couch and patting the cushion next to him. "Come sit with me, will you?"

She looked down at him and almost laughed seeing that the black eye she'd given him was just starting to heal and now he had a shiner on the other eye to match, making him look like a raccoon.

"Thank you for coming to my rescue tonight," she said, sitting down next to him.

"Why were you even in Burley's after I told you I didn't want you there?"

"Zeb Taylor, you can't tell me what to do. Especially since you never tell me what you're doing."

He seemed to think it over and then nodded. "All right. Fair enough. I'm sorry that I haven't acted the way you would have liked lately but –"

"I know what you're going to say. You're a bachelor and you can't change your ways. Don't bother telling me."

"That's not what I was going to say."

"Then what is it, Zeb? Are you going to try to deny that you made dates with those two girls while we were married?"

She heard him sigh, then his hand went up to touch his hurt eyes and he looked the other way when he spoke. "No. I'm not going to deny it, but that's not exactly how it went. I didn't make the date while we were married. I just postponed it, that's all. At the time, I had my mind set on being a bachelor and didn't think we were going to stay married anyway. Still, I know it was wrong, and I am sorry. I just wasn't sure I wanted to be married, but now I've changed my mind."

"Oh really?" Her stomach lurched. She'd had so much to drink that she felt like she had to vomit. "I can't listen to anything more tonight, Zeb." She started to walk away but he grabbed her arm to stop her.

"Please, Cat, let me explain."

"Zeb, if you don't let go of me, you're going to be sorry."

"I'm not going to let go of you. Ever."

Cat tried to get away but she couldn't. Nor could she stop herself from hurling her insides, just turning her head to miss Zeb, but still throwing-up all over his shoes.

"Are you sick, sweetie?" he asked. "Here, lie on the couch while I clean up."

She was asleep before her head even hit the couch pillow.

CHAPTER 22

Zeb waited patiently for Cat to wake up the next morning, having already gone over in his head a hundred times what he was going to say to her. He'd planned on telling her all about her brother, but then Lorenzo called earlier and told him he'd decided to go home and get some sleep last night since there were no stand-bys to be had. Fortunately, he was able to board a plane this morning and it had already landed at Kalamazoo airport. Zeb had phoned Nate to go pick him up at the airport and to bring him directly over to their lake house.

Lorenzo asked him not to say anything yet because he decided to surprise Cat, after all. Now, Zeb just hoped he could avoid her question of where he'd been until Lorenzo got there.

"Wake up, sweetheart," he said, pushing a lock of her long, dark hair behind her ear. "How are you feeling?"

She stretched and opened her eyes and actually smiled at him, probably forgetting how much she really hated him for a second.

"Zeb?" she asked, then made a face as she tasted the inside of her mouth and she remembered just what happened last night. "Oh, no. I'm sorry I threw up on you."

"It's all right, Cat," he said. "I'll get a new pair of shoes. Now, why don't you go brush your teeth because I have somewhere to take you."

"I can't go anywhere before I shower and put on some make-up," she said, making her way to the bathroom.

"Cat, please. This is important. No one is going to see us. Just brush your teeth and come with me. It won't take long."

"Oh, all right," she said and disappeared into the bathroom and closed the door.

Zeb waited nervously for her to come out of the bathroom, going over in his head what he was going to say when he asked her to marry him. He had a box wrapped up in his back pocket with a ruby necklace in it that he'd bought for her at the airport while he was waiting for a flight. It was expensive and also lined with diamonds. He knew he was taking a chance that she might not accept it since she'd think he was throwing his money around again to get her to forgive him, but it was a chance he had to take.

He wanted to use the rings from Vegas again just as a token until they had time to go shopping for real rings, but hell if he could remember what he did with his, nor did he ever know what Cat did with hers.

So this morning, since it was the weekend and Thomas' kids were home from school, he sent Dan and Sam over to his office to look through his desk drawers for the ring. He heard car tires on the gravel outside and looked out the window to see Dan's '67 Chevy convertible pulling down the driveway. He ran out to greet them.

"Dan, Sam, did you find my ring?" he asked anxiously, running up to their car.

"Sorry, Uncle Zeb," said Dan shaking his head. "We looked everywhere but couldn't find it."

"Maybe it's under some of the papers on my desk. It's pretty messy. Did you look there?"

"It wasn't messy at all," said Sam. "Ever since Cat cleaned it, everything is organized and in the file cabinet. You should see it. She did a great job."

"Yeah," said Dan. "For a while there, we thought we had the wrong office."

"Cat did that?" he asked, feeling his heart go out to her. She'd been working so hard to make things nice for him. The fact she'd furnished the cottage with antiques and also decorated it didn't go unnoticed either. She had been trying so hard to make this marriage work and, unfortunately, he had done nothing to add to the relationship at all. If they weren't already married, he had no doubt in his mind that Cat would probably turn down his proposal. "All right, thanks, boys. Now, you'd better get going because Cat is coming out and I'm going to take her for a rowboat ride and propose to her."

"Sweet," said Dan and turned the car around. They were just about to drive away when they stopped and Sam called out to him.

"Oh, Uncle Zeb, this was on your desk and it looked important so we thought we'd better bring it to you."

Zeb walked over and grabbed the letter from Sam, seeing that it looked like his annulment papers.

"Was it already opened?" he asked, studying the envelope.

"Yep. Maybe Cat did it, but it wasn't us," said Sam as the car rolled away down the driveway.

Zeb took one look at the Decree of Annulment signed by the judge, realizing he was no longer married to Cat. All records of them ever being husband and wife were null and void. This hit him hard in the gut, as it wasn't what he wanted to see just now. Damn, he never should have paid extra to push it through so quickly. He regretted it now, not realizing at the time what a mistake he was making. If the letter was opened, then Cat obviously had seen it, too.

"Okay, I'm ready. Where are we going?" asked Cat, coming down the stairs to meet him. She had changed and thrown on some makeup, after all. He smiled inwardly knowing that Cat was so much like him that there was no doubt in his mind they belonged together. He usually didn't go out the door before he looked his best either, but things had changed. Now he was walking around with stubble on his face and two black eyes. Although he'd changed his clothes and shoes, he swore he still smelled from last night's puke.

He took the letter and held it up for her to see it. "Did you open this?" he asked, and saw her eyes dart the other way.

"Yes, I did," she admitted.

"Cat, how do you feel about no longer being married?"

He had hoped she'd tell him she hated it and wanted to stay married, but instead she acted nonchalant.

"It doesn't matter," she said, looking out toward the lake. "So, are we going somewhere or what?"

"Yes. Come with me."

CAT WENT with Zeb down to the lake, wondering what this was all about. She figured since he had the letter in his hand and asked her how she felt about not being married any more, that this was all leading up to that big news he had about where he'd been lately. It hurt her more than anything to think of Zeb with someone else, but she didn't want to let him know that. That's why she acted as if she didn't care.

"Judas said Denny and his friends were wanted in Vegas and that they'll be behind bars for a long time."

"What about me?" she asked, stopping in her tracks. "I cheated for that scum. Are they going to put me in jail as well?"

"No, you're not going to jail, Cat. I made sure of that."

"How? Why? What did you do?"

"I made sure they knew you were being forced to do what Denny wanted. However, down the line, you may have to testify against the man."

"My pleasure. I'll do whatever it takes to put him behind bars where he belongs."

They stopped walking and were now on the pier. Cat looked down to see a rowboat. Zeb untied it and got inside. The waves moved the boat up and down, already making her feel dizzy.

"Come on. Get in, Cat."

"You want me to get in that thing? You've got to be kidding. I don't even like the water."

"Please. I have something I need to ask you. I thought we could row out to the middle of the lake and that it would be . . . I don't know. Romantic."

Cat didn't know what Zeb was up to, but he almost sounded as if he wanted to make amends so she figured she'd give it a shot. She stepped out to get into the boat, but became dizzy and put her foot and weight on the side of the boat instead.

"No! That's not how you get into a boat!" she heard him shout. But it was too late. She tilted the boat and lost her balance, and ended up dumping both of them into the water.

She would have been upset by it, but when she saw Zeb sitting in the lake looking like a drowned rat, she burst out laughing.

"It's not funny," he said, spitting water from his mouth. He crawled out of the lake and helped her to her feet. They both made it to the pier and sat down. Zeb pulled off his shoes and water poured out as he laid them one by one on the pier next to them.

"Oh, Zeb, I'm going to miss you. I'm sorry things didn't work out in our marriage."

"What are you talking about?" he asked.

"I know what's going on," she said. "You went to St. Louis to be with a girl. Don't try to hide the fact. Remember, I called and the woman answered."

Now it was his turn to laugh, though Cat didn't think it was funny.

"Sweetheart, that's not why I was there. That woman you

heard on the phone was only the wife of a man I went to see. She just happened to answer."

"Oh. Really?"

"I swear. It's true. I'll also tell you exactly what I was doing there and who I was meeting, but first I have to tell you that I love you."

"You . . . love me?" Cat never expected to hear him say this.

"I love you and I want you to marry me, even if our annulment already went through because I was too unorganized to stop the procedure."

"You mean you didn't do that on purpose?"

"Of course not, Cat. Sweetheart, I realize that you were right about everything. I do like my toys too much and the things money can buy."

"Then don't give them up, Zeb. I have to admit I like them, too. You were right about me using my looks to get what I want, after all."

"So, you're saying that you don't care if I keep my designer clothes, the Mercedes, or even Jeeva?"

"I don't mind at all." She reached up and touched him gently on his cheek. "I saw how miserable you were when we tried the contest, and I admit I was just as miserable. Face it. Neither of us could even continue the contest only after one day. Why put ourselves through that misery again? I know that your aunt was right now in stopping me from marrying James and tricking me into marrying you. After all, we really do belong together."

"Good ol' Aunt Cappy. I'll have to thank her later. For now, Cat, I want to tell you that I love you and I want to marry you. For real this time." He slipped off the pier and got down on his knees in the water and took her hand in his. "I don't have a ring, because I wanted to let you pick it out yourself. However, I did get you something to hold us over."

He handed her a long box and she opened it. Water came sloshing out and landed on her lap and made her jerk backwards.

They both laughed at that. She looked down to see the most beautiful necklace she'd ever seen made from rubies and diamonds.

"Zeb, it's beautiful," she said in awe. "It must have cost you a fortune."

"I'm not trying to bribe you with expensive gifts like you think, sweetheart. I just can't help myself. I like nice things and that's one of the reasons I like you. Cat, you deserve this, as well as so much more than I could ever give you. I love you, and want to be with you for the rest of my life."

"Zeb, do you really mean it?" Cat didn't want to jinx it, but had to be sure.

"I do."

"Tell me more of those reasons why you love me."

"I love the way you smile, sweetheart. Your face lights up and makes my heart sing. And, of course, I love the way you look. Your eyes are like mirrors to your soul and your lips are so seductive that I just can't help it –" he shot forward and plastered a big kiss on her, surprising her again. "I just have to kiss you."

"Go on," she said playfully, giving him one of her seductive glances.

"You cleaned my desk and organized my office, and I love you for it. I noticed the way you also fixed up our new house."

"Our new house? Does this mean you're not hell-bent on still living in the condo in Benton Harbor?"

"Not anymore. I understand now how important it is to be near our family. We can fix up the cabin however we want, and maybe even remodel and expand it."

"Maybe Jeeva can move in with us, too," she suggested. Zeb looked happy to hear he wouldn't have to give up his virtual maid, after all. "Just as long as you don't have her calling you master anymore," she added with a smile.

"I promise," he said, giving her a smile of his own that warmed her heart. He looked so sexy, even with his two black eyes. "Cat, there are a ton more things I love about you, but I have to know something first. Will you marry me and make me the happiest man in the world?"

"You're sure you're willing to give up being a bachelor? Forever?"

"Damned sure. Now what's your answer?"

She couldn't tease him any more. She believed everything he had just said and knew it was time to stop being afraid of the good things in her life turning bad. She felt the same way about Zeb that he felt about her.

"I know I said a lot of hurtful things to you, Zeb, and I'm sorry. I've realized lately that I have some pretty strong feelings for you as well. I love being in Sweetwater and on Thunder Lake and around your family. It's the family I always wanted, and you are the man I always dreamed of, even if I didn't know it at first. I want to spend the rest of my life with you, Zebedee Taylor. I love you, too. Yes! I will marry you and be your wife."

He clasped the necklace on her and took her hands in his and kissed her.

"Yahoo!" she shouted, as he picked her up off the pier, kissing her in the process. Then he lost his footing and they both fell into the lake again, laughing.

"Am I interrupting anything?" came a voice from the shore.

She looked up to see a tall, dark-haired man standing there with Nate next to him. Suddenly, she was a child again. And when the man smiled, she knew exactly who he was and her heart swelled with joy. But this couldn't be so, could it? She was afraid to believe it was true. Her brother was dead, so how could he be standing in front of her right now?

"Lorenzo?" she asked softly, her voice shaking, as she saw the ghost of her brother returning from the grave. "Is that really you?"

"Cat, that's where I've been," Zeb explained, helping her up out of the water. "I've been searching for your brother. I had a feeling that if your father was as devious as you said he was, that he might have lied about your brother's death."

"That's right," added Lorenzo. "Father told me that you and Mom were dead as well."

Cat couldn't move at first. Her hand went to her mouth and tears welled in her eyes. Her lips trembled.

"Go to him, sweetheart," said Zeb, helping her from the water and giving her a gentle nudge forward. She ran to her brother who she hadn't seen in nearly twenty years and hugged him, laying her head on his chest. She was all wet, but neither of them cared.

"This is too good to be true," she cried, reaching up and kissing Lorenzo on the cheek, all the while sobbing with tears of joy. "You are alive! We're together again," she said, pulling back to take a good look at her brother.

"It's all because of Zeb." Lorenzo nodded to Zeb who was still standing in the water.

Cat's heart swelled with love. She ran back over to Zeb again and kissed him and hugged him and then hit him in the arm. He held a hand up to cover his face and smiled.

"Please don't slug me again," he begged her. "I already look like a raccoon."

"Oh, Zeb, I'm sorry. I'm sorry for accusing you of being with other women and I'm sorry I almost ruined our marriage. Thank you so much for finding my brother and for asking me to marry you. This is all a dream come true and I don't want it to ever end."

"It's not going to end, Cat, I'll make damned sure of that," Zeb promised. "This is just the beginning of our life together. Now, how about we all go inside and get dry? Nate, maybe you can invite the rest of the family over here to help us celebrate because Cat has just agreed to marry me."

"Again?" asked Nate.

"Again," Zeb repeated, pulling Cat into his arms. "And this time, I swear it's going to last forever."

* * *

AN HOUR LATER, everyone was filing into Cat's new home and she had never felt happier in her life. Zeb and her brother were on the deck barbecuing and drinking beer with Zeb's brothers, Levi and Nate. Judas sat next to his daughter googling over his grandson and trying to learn as much as he could about being a father before his new baby was born.

All the kids were out in the front lawn playing. Dan, Thomas' eldest son, was flirting with J.D.'s friend, Charlotte, who they'd invited over as well.

"Cat, we're so happy for you," said Angel, helping to put food into serving dishes. Since this was on such short notice, Candace had suggested they bring side salads over from the diner and grill burgers and brats.

"Yes," said Laney. "Not only are you engaged but you found your long-lost brother who you thought was dead."

"Someone pinch me and tell me this is all real," said Cat, "because I cannot believe that something this good is really happening to me."

"It's real. So, believe it," said Angel.

"How are you feeling with the morning sickness?" Cat asked Laney.

"Better, but I swear sometimes I feel seasick."

"Honey, the burgers and brats are almost done," said Zeb, popping his head in through the open sliding glass doors. "Can you bring me a platter?"

"Sure," said Cat, taking the platter out to the porch. She looked down to the lawn where the kids were playing and noticed that Zeb had taken not only his wet clothes from the lake but also his wet money from his pocket and hung it up to dry with clothes pins from the thin branches of a lilac tree. "What's that?" she asked with a giggle, seeing his money blowing back and forth in the summer breeze. The younger kids were trying to jump up and touch it.

"I'm laundering money," he said with a smile. Cat reached over and kissed him.

"Funny," she said.

"Yeah, but too bad I'm also into laundering cell phones," he told her.

She realized his cell phone had fallen into the water as well and felt bad that it was ruined. Then she heard her phone ringing from inside the house and ran to answer it.

"Hello?" she said, not recognizing the number.

"Cat? Where is everyone?"

"Who is this?" she asked.

"It's James. I'm over at Thomas' cabin. I've unloaded my horses and I tried calling all of my brothers but no one is answering."

"James?" Now this could be awkward, but Cat knew she'd have to face it sooner or later. "Zeb's phone fell in the lake and the rest of us are at our new cabin. Zeb asked me to marry him and I said yes. We're having a barbecue to celebrate."

"I thought you were already married," he said in confusion.

"Well, we were and then we weren't. But this time, it's going to be for real."

"Oh," was all he said, and then was very quiet.

"We'd like you to come join us if you could. We're across the channel from Thomas' main house, and a few houses down from Judas and Laney's. Just look for the crowd and listen for the noise and you'll find us."

"Are you sure I should come?" he asked cautiously.

"James, I know it might be a little awkward, but you're going to be my brother-in-law now. I am in love with Zeb. So please, come be part of the family."

"Ok, I'll be right there," he said, clicking off the phone.

"I've got to go, Sis," said Lorenzo. "My wife just called and she's in labor." Lorenzo kissed Cat quickly and ran out the door with Nate.

"Wait!" she called after him. "When will I see you again?"

"Talk to Zeb, he'll tell you everything."

Zeb walked up to her with a bratwurst in his hand, taking a bite and then offering her a bite as well.

"No, thanks," she said, pushing it away. The smell of it, or maybe just all the excitement had her feeling a little queasy again. "When will my brother be back?" she asked.

"Well, as soon as they have the baby, sell their place, and pack up his office, I guess."

"What does that mean?" She felt a tingle of excitement rush through her.

"It means Lorenzo is going to be working for me now. He's agreed to rent my condo until they can find a place to live."

"That's wonderful," cried Cat. "Oh, Zeb, I can hardly wait. I feel that, for the first time in my life, I'm going to have a real family."

"Uncle James!" one of the kids called out. Cat looked up to see Zeb's twin brother, James, riding up to their house on a horse. Five other horses were tethered together, following right behind him.

"James!" Zeb finished eating the brat in two bites and walked over to greet his brother.

"Who wants to ride my horses?" James called out, tipping his cowboy hat to Cat in the process. He slid off the horse and handed the reins to Dan. All the kids jumped and yelled and shouted out that they wanted to ride the horses he'd brought with him from Texas.

"Congrats on your engagement," said James, taking off his hat and shaking his brother's hand. "You, too, Cat," he said with a nod.

"Oh, come here you goof and give me a hug. We're going to be family," Cat told him.

After they hugged, Zeb looked at his brother. "Are you ok with all this, Bro?"

"Sure," said James, nodding his head. "But just to let you know, you better never treat Catalina poorly or you'll have hell to pay with me."

"You'll find someone for you, James," said Cat. "Just give it some time."

"Are you going to be staying with Thomas until you find somewhere to live?" asked Zeb.

"He offered," said James, "but I think I'm going to look for a farm with more room for the horses. His barn is too small and my horses need an open field to run and graze. I hear Old Man MacAllister is getting on in years and looking for help running his farm. Word is he's looking for a boarder, or at least that's what Gus told me when I stopped by his gas station on the way in. MacAllister has a big barn that'll house all my horses. I'm going to go see him about it in the morning."

"James," said Zeb. "I wanted to ask you – that is, if Cat doesn't mind – to be my best man at the wedding. It would mean a lot to me if you did."

"Do you mind?" James asked Cat.

"Not at all," she said with a smile. "I would be honored."

"Then I accept," he said and finally smiled. Cat had been starting to wonder if he would ever smile again.

"Who is going to be your maid of honor?" asked Aunt Cappy, walking up to them, having overheard the entire conversation. Laney was at her side.

"Well, Laney, you've become my best friend since I've been in Sweetwater so I'd like to ask you," said Cat. "However, I really have to ask Aunt Cappy to be my maid of honor as well since she was the reason behind us getting married in the first place."

"I accept. I'd be thrilled to be your matron of honor," said Laney.

"I'd love to do it, too," said Aunt Cappy with a huge smile. She let out a deep sigh. "Always a bridesmaid and never a bride."

"Aunt Cappy, don't even try to pretend," said Zeb with a grin. "We all know you were never a bridesmaid and always a bride."

"That's what I meant to say," she corrected herself with a giggle. "Never a bridesmaid, always a bride."

"Zeb, there's someone on the phone who wants to congratulate you," said Levi, walking up and handing his cell phone to Zeb.

ZEB TOOK THE PHONE, not at all sure of who would be calling to congratulate him because most his family was already here.

"Hello, who is this?" asked Zeb.

"Ahoy, matey," he heard from the other end and knew at once it was his brother, Simon. "Congrats, I hear you're getting married."

"Thanks, Simon. Where are you?"

"I'm still in the Caribbean. Since I enjoy sailing so much, I've been working as safety officer aboard a luxury liner cruise ship."

"Well, I hope you can come home for our wedding," said Zeb. "Be sure to bring our no-good bum of a brother, Thad, with you when you come."

"Well, that depends when it is. Have you set a date yet?" Simon asked him.

"Not yet, but I think Cat would agree with me that it'll be as soon as possible. Maybe next week if we can work it all out. Neither of us want to wait." He looked up and winked at Cat.

"Well, I won't be able to make that. But tell me, have you planned a honeymoon at all?"

"We haven't even discussed it, but I want to take Cat somewhere nice. I want it to be romantic."

"Then I have the perfect idea. I want you two to be the guests of honor and spend your honeymoon aboard the Seduction of the Seas."

"The Seduction of the Seas?" asked Zeb, thinking this sounded like it was made for them.

"Yes, it's the name of the cruise ship I'm employed on right now. Come have your honeymoon here. My treat. I'll even make sure you get the honeymoon suite and the whole elaborate package. Thad will be here as well."

"Well, that sounds good to me. Let me ask Cat."

"Yes!" she said from right behind him, having had her ear close to the phone and listening to the whole conversation. "I've never been on a cruise, Zeb. I would love to go. Especially since the ship is called Seduction. It's perfect for us, don't you agree?"

"All right then," said Zeb with a chuckle, thinking how wonderful this all sounded. "When does the ship leave port?"

"A week from tomorrow. Can you make it?"

He pulled Cat to him and she snuggled against his chest. Then he kissed her atop the head. "We'll be there," he told him. "A cruise is perfect because Catalina and I are going to be enjoying our honeymoon to the fullest."

CHAPTER 23

*I*t was a week later and Cat nervously waited in the enclosed glass sun porch of Thomas and Angel's house for the wedding to start. Her head was spinning from making all their wedding plans so fast. Since they were only required to wait three days after getting their marriage license before they could actually wed, Zeb's entire family pitched in to help however they could and everything was working out perfectly.

She'd talked it over with Zeb and they decided since they were going on a luxurious honeymoon that they would both try to change their ways a little. They planned a small, hometown wedding with the immediate family and some close friends instead of the huge, expensive one they both really wanted to have.

Nate had put a down payment on Burley's Bar since it was for sale again, and at a very cheap price. With Zeb's professional help to rush through the closing, he was now the new proprietor. Nate offered the bar for the reception but Cat and Zeb had decided it was too dark and gloomy. Instead, they had tents with tables and chairs set up on the huge lawn in front of Thomas' house where they would have an outdoor wedding and reception.

"Cat, the music's starting," said Laney, walking into the sun porch with Aunt Cappy who had a bouquet of flowers in her hands. Aunt Cappy had the local florist in Kalamazoo make them up and they consisted of white and red roses with glitter-sprinkled baby's breath. They matched the ruby and diamond necklace Zeb gave Cat. She had been wearing it all the time and would cherish it forever.

Zeb told her they could pick out nice wedding rings, but with everything going on and Zeb trying to take care of his clients this week as well as help Nate with the bar, they just hadn't had the time. They ended up deciding to just use the rings they'd been married with in Vegas until they could find replacements. Cat still had hers, as well as Zeb's from the day she found it on the sink.

"The yard looks wonderful," said Laney. "You were so lucky that it is a beautiful day and it didn't rain."

"Let's keep that thought," said Cat, trying not to break her good luck streak. She had a new outlook on life now. Since she'd been attending Laney's meditations, she discovered how to still her mind and stay positive. "Thanks for all the help," Cat told her. "If it wasn't for you two and Angel and Candace, I don't know what we'd have done."

"You would have gotten married in the church like my brother would have wanted, and then had your reception at the diner just like everyone else in this family," said Cappy in a scolding manner.

"I know you're not happy about our choice, Aunt Cappy, but Zeb and I wanted to do something different from his brothers. Besides, it is so beautiful by the lake and there is much more room for everyone outside. Plus, the kids don't have to sit still the entire time. I want to say thank you both again for standing up for my wedding. Aunt Cappy, you being my maid of honor along with Laney is special to me because, lately, you have been reminding me a lot of my mother."

"I hope that's a good thing, dear," she said.

"A very good thing," Cat answered, feeling the presence of her mother in the room every time Aunt Cappy was near.

Just then, Cat's brother, Lorenzo, walked into the room with a smile on his face and a baby in his arms.

"Lorenzo! You made it for the wedding." Cat ran over and hugged her brother.

"I wouldn't miss it for the world, Sister. Cat, I want you to meet the newest member of the family, Rose." Lorenzo's wife and daughter followed him into the room and Cat greeted them as well, as this was the first time she'd ever met them.

"You named the baby Rose?" Cat looked down to the little baby girl in his arms. "She's precious. You named her after our mother."

"I wanted our mother's spirit to live on through my daughter," said Lorenzo. "I wish I had known her as well as you did, but we can't go back and change the past."

"Are you going to walk me down the aisle?" Cat asked, feeling an emptiness inside her of not having had a father to love and give her away on this special day.

"Of course," he said, handing his baby to his wife who took their children and headed back out to join the rest of the crowd. "Cat, although I know our father did some bad things and you still hate him, I want you to know that he was good to me. He's gone now, and you need to forgive him and move on."

"I know you're right, Lorenzo. I will try, I promise I will."

"We all make mistakes," he told her. "As long as we learn from them, that's all that really matters."

"Yes, you're right and I think I am living proof of that." Cat thought about all the mistakes she'd made in her life and how Zeb accepted her without judging her past. He loved her for who she was and she loved him also and wasn't going to try to change anything about him ever again.

Nate's band started playing a unique version of the wedding march, and Cat followed Laney and Aunt Cappy outside, holding on to the arm of her brother. Her stomach started twitching again and she figured her nerves were starting to get the best of her. She just hoped she wouldn't get sick on Zeb on their wedding day.

ZEB LOOKED up across the lawn to see the most beautiful girl in the world making her way toward him. Cat wore a sleeveless, long, white, lace, wedding gown with a low neckline trimmed in small pearls. She looked so sexy showing her cleavage, and he had to admit that he liked it. Her hair was left long, just the way Zeb liked it, hanging down past her breasts. Her nails were done in a French tip and her makeup was subtler than when he'd first met her in the casino. Now, she looked more natural. As a matter of fact, Zeb thought she looked as if she were glowing.

She was so beautiful that she didn't need makeup or fancy baubles, though the necklace he'd given her did look impressive around her neck.

He looked at the crowd on the front lawn and smiled. It was mostly just Zeb's brothers and their families, but they had invited a few extra guests from town such as Mrs. Durnsby, Gus from the gas station and his family, and Charlotte, J.D.'s best friend.

Cat had managed to take a simple lawn and make it look elegant. They had canopy-type tents set up with tables and chairs inside that were wrapped with white cloth and big, red bows. Vases of wildflowers were atop each table. Zeb and his brothers had built a raised platform for Nate's band, as well as a small wooden arbor that they were going to stand under to get married. It, too, was decorated with flowers, ribbons and bows and was painted a bright white with yellow trim.

Cat had a knack for decorating, and Zeb was impressed by all her talents that he'd recently just found out she had.

Lorenzo stopped in front of the preacher and handed Cat over to Zeb. The music stopped as well. Zeb had an overwhelming feeling of love in his heart. He looked over to his best man and twin brother, James, who was wearing his cowboy hat with his tux. It almost made Zeb laugh aloud. Zeb wore a black tux as well, with a white shirt and red bowtie. Laney stood to the side next to James, and Aunt Cappy fussed with Cat's hair.

Zeb looked over to the front row where his brothers, Thomas, Levi, and Judas were standing with their wives and their many children.

He wished the rest of his brothers could have been here, but he also realized it was short notice. He and Cat didn't want to wait to be married the second time around. Although this wedding might have been rushed, it was not nearly as rushed as going to a drive-thru chapel.

"Are you ready?" asked Reverend Black, the pastor from the Twelve Apostles nondenominational church, looking over the top of his bifocals with the prayer book in his hand.

Zeb looked over to Cat and smiled. "We're ready," he said.

The appropriate prayers were said and when it came time for the vows, they had written their own.

Cat was first, and he listened intently.

"Zeb, I can't wait to spend the rest of my life with you," she said. "I know I was very manipulative with my ways when we first met, but I feel as if I've changed since we've been married – the first time," she said and laughter went up from the crowd. "I don't want to change you, because I love you just the way you are."

"Even with two black eyes?" he asked, and again a laugh went up from the crowd.

"Especially with two black eyes," she told him. "After all, it shows what we've been through. I gave you one black eye and the other you got defending me. Thank you, for everything. I will be so happy to be your wife."

Next, it was Zeb's turn to say something. He took her hands in his and stared deeply into her eyes. "Cat, I know our road has been rocky. But together, we can pave the way to our future. I look forward to growing old with you and to raising a family with you as well. I know I've lived a life that most people would think is reckless and crude, but I'm willing to change however I can so we can start a new life together."

"Don't change too much, though," she said, her hand going to her ruby and diamond necklace.

The crowd chuckled again and then it was time for the rings.

James stepped forward and pulled a small box from his pocket. He opened it and took out two rings and dropped them into Zeb's hand.

"These aren't our rings," Zeb said, looking down to his hand to see the ornate gold and diamond wedding rings James had bought when he thought he was marrying Cat instead.

"I know," said James. "But I want you two to have them."

"James?" asked Cat, looking up to Zeb's brother. "Are you sure?"

"Use them for now," he said. "If you decide you want to sell them and replace them later, I won't mind."

"I don't know," said Zeb, thinking maybe James was still wishing it were him being married to Cat. "I'm not sure this is a good idea."

"Zeb, you are my twin brother," said James. "We've shared our looks, our clothes, and . . . even our girlfriends in the past." Again a chuckle from the crowd. "I know you and Cat are in love and that you two were meant for each other. I'm more of a simple kind of man and Cat is more complex and enjoys being surrounded by the finer things in life, like you. It never would have worked out between us. I have no hard feelings about any of this. I love you both, as family and nothing more. Now, please accept the rings as my token of appreciation to have such a wonderful brother and now a wonderful sister-in-law, too."

"Well," said Zeb, running his hand over the back of his head. "What do you think, Cat?"

She looked up and smiled at James, then looked to Zeb and nodded slightly. "I think you're lucky to have a brother like James and that we should accept his gift because it came from his heart."

"Not to mention, you really paid for those rings at the poker table anyway," James reminded Zeb with a smile.

"That's true," Zeb agreed. "All right, then," he said, taking Cat's hand in his and glancing over at the preacher. "Just keep this short and simple," he whispered.

"Of course," Reverend Black whispered back. "Repeat after me."

The vows were said and the rings exchanged, and then the preacher made the announcement. "I now pronounce you man and wife. Everyone, let's congratulate the new Mr. and Mrs. Zebedee Taylor." The crowd clapped and cheered and then the preacher looked back at Zeb. "You may now kiss the bride."

"Now this part, I've been waiting for," he said, pulling Cat into his arms and kissing her passionately – much too passionately to be doing it in front of everyone.

"Oh my!" he heard the ex-mayor, Mrs. Durnsby, gasp.

"Get a room," shouted out Nate, breaking the tension. The crowd cheered and clapped for the new couple once again.

Then Cat threw her bouquet over her shoulder and it slammed into Aunt Cappy's big bosom.

"Oh!" Cappy cried out, catching the bouquet. "I don't want this! I've been married enough times already." She tossed it out to the crowd and Judas' daughter, J.D., ended up catching it and holding it up proudly in one hand while holding her baby in the other.

"I got it," J.D. said happily, lifting it high to show her best friend, Charlotte, who was standing next to her.

"Good, now maybe you'll get a husband to help you raise that baby," grumbled Judas.

"You know that means we'll have to pay for a big wedding," Laney reminded him.

"Throw it back, quick!" Judas called out, causing everyone to laugh. The music started up again and the people came forward to congratulate the newlyweds. Levi popped a cork from a champagne bottle and filled up two glasses and gave them to Zeb and Cat.

"Make a toast," someone shouted. Zeb held his glass high to do just that.

"To a wonderful wife, a wonderful honeymoon, and many children," said Zeb. Glasses clinked together and Zeb had no idea at the time that he'd get everything he wished for – and quicker than he thought.

he next day, Zeb celebrated with his new wife aboard the cruise ship, the Seduction of the Seas, with his brother Simon and also his youngest brother, Thad.

"It's so good to see you again," he said to his brothers as they leaned on the railing and looked out over the sea. He was waiting for his new bride to come join them, and had noticed that Cat was seasick already. He was starting to wonder if they should have planned a different honeymoon since she really didn't care for boats or water that much to begin with.

"Zeb, I'm glad you decided to take the cruise," said Simon, leaning over the railing and perusing the sea. He looked a lot like Zeb and James and was born less than a year after them. While growing up, people referred to Simon as the Irish twin – or Irish triplet in this case. He very well could have been a triplet with the way he resembled Zeb and James, except that Simon had bright blue eyes the color of the sea and was built like a brick shit house. "I love the sea," Simon said, taking a deep breath and releasing it and getting this odd look on his face that almost made Zeb laugh.

"What's with the face?" Zeb asked.

"That's his pirate's face," said Thad from next to him. Thad was the youngest of the Taylor boys at only twenty-four years of age. He had gone through some hard times with substance abuse back in high school, and was an Irish twin with his brother, Nate. The two of them were less than a year apart in age. Thad's body was covered with colorful tattoos on his arms, and his blond hair was shaved short on the sides and was long and spiked over to one side in the center. "Simon always gets that stink face when he's lost to the sea."

The breeze blew against them and Simon put a quick hand on his uniform captain-type hat to keep from losing it. He looked proud in his seaman's uniform that identified him as one of the ship's crew. Zeb knew Simon was proud of having been a navy man though he was no longer enlisted.

Zeb figured Simon hadn't come home yet because he not only loved the sea, but was probably watching over Thad as well. Thad was a man now and in control of his life and didn't need watching over, but Simon always seemed to mother him ever since he was born.

"I'm here now," said Cat, coming to join them with a big smile on her face.

"We're so glad to have you in our family," Thad told her and Simon agreed.

"Thanks, guys," she said. "So, when will you two be returning to Sweetwater to claim your inheritance?"

"Well, funny you should ask," said Simon, pulling his gaze from the water. "Actually, Thad and I have been talking about that since we found out you two were getting married."

"I'm ready to go home now," said Thad, being the quieter of the two. "I was angry when I found out Ma had Alzheimer's and even angrier when I heard she'd died."

"Is that why you didn't come home for the funeral?" asked Zeb.

Thad just nodded. "I guess I didn't want to accept it."

"We're both coming back now," said Simon with a nod. "This

will be my last cruise aboard the ship. My job ended almost before it began, but I decided family is more important than anything in life and that I need to move back to the Sweetwater area."

"That's great news!" said Zeb, slapping Simon on the back. "Isn't it, sweetheart?" He looked over at Cat and she was making a funny face. The next thing he knew, she hung her head over the railing and emptied the contents of her stomach into the sea.

"Cat?" asked Zeb, starting to realize that it wasn't seasickness that was bringing this on. "Is there something you want to tell me?"

Simon snagged a napkin from a waiter walking by and handed it to her. She wiped her mouth then looked up to Zeb and nodded.

"I went to see the ship's doctor this morning, and he gave me a test to take back to my cabin."

"A test?" asked Thad.

"A stick you pee on," Zeb growled. "Do we need to explain everything to you, Thad?"

"That's right," said Cat before Thad could respond, obviously wanting to intervene before there was a riff between the brothers. "Anyway – I didn't pass the test."

"You mean . . . you mean . . ." If Zeb had had a hard time saying the M word, he certainly was having a hard time saying the B word now.

"She's pregnant!" It was Thad's turn to insult his big brother. "You do know what that means . . . a baby?"

"A b . . . b . . . b . . ."

"Baby!" Cat, Thad, and Simon said together.

"What's that face you're making?" asked Simon.

"It's either his bachelor face or his stupid face," said Thad. "Either one isn't very admirable, especially with those black eyes."

"Yep, I'm pregnant, Zeb," Cat confirmed. "It's still very early and I can't believe it happened so fast, but the doctor told me it's true. We're going to have a baby."

Zeb just stood there with his mouth open, not sure what to say.

"Close your mouth, Brother," said Simon. "With those black eyes and gaping mouth, you're starting to remind me of a grouper I caught last week."

"Sweetie, are you happy about this?" Cat asked Zeb, looking at him curiously.

"I'm elated, and I must admit a little shocked." Zeb pulled her to him and gave her a hug, kissing her atop the head.

"Just think, now we'll be having a baby the same time as everyone else back home," Cat pointed out.

"So, it looks like you two had a little honeymoon before the honeymoon, didn't you?" asked Thad.

"No," said Cat, raising her chin with a smile on her full lips. "I wouldn't call it a honeymoon that did this. I'd say it was just the results of the fine art of **Seducing Zeb**."

FROM THE AUTHOR

I hope you enjoyed **Seducing Zeb – Book 4**, in the **Tarnished Saints Series.** These twelve brothers are trouble all right, and writing their stories is a challenge, because they have minds of their own.

For example, I had every intention on having Cat and Zeb retire from their elaborate ways of living, but they really didn't want to. So, we came to a happy medium where I let them keep the clothes and the car and the perks of doing whatever they wanted with their money. However, I made them live in the lake house by Zeb's brothers and give up the condo. Of course, we all know that won't be good enough for either of them. In the next book, you'll see the plans they've made for improving their cottage in *Saving Simon – Book 5.*

Many incidents in my own life are what inspired this series. I grew up visiting my grandparents on a small lake in Michigan. The incident with Cat and Zeb falling in the lake and Zeb hanging his money in the tree to dry was something that actually happened to my parents. I love putting things like this into my books, because that way my memories will live on forever.

This is a twelve-book series and in case if you've missed any of the first books, I've listed them all for you.

Tarnished Saints' Christmas – Prequel
Doubting Thomas *– Book 1*
Luring Levi *– Book 2*
Judging Judas *– Book 3*
Seducing Zeb *– Book 4*
Saving Simon *– Book 5*
Wrangling James *– Book 6*
Praising Pete *– Book 7*
Teaching Philip *– Book 8*
Loving John – Book 9
Playing Nate – Book 10
Igniting Andrew – Book 11
Taming Thad – Book 12

Thank you!

Elizabeth Rose

ABOUT ELIZABETH

Elizabeth Rose is a multi-published, bestselling author, writing medieval, historical, contemporary, paranormal, and western romance. Her books are available as EBooks, paperbacks, and audiobooks as well.

Her favorite characters in her works include dark, dangerous and tortured heroes, and feisty, independent heroines who know how to wield a sword. She loves writing 14th century medieval novels, and is well-known for her many series.

Her twelve-book small town contemporary series, Tarnished Saints, was inspired by incidents in her own life.

After being traditionally published, she started self-publishing, creating her own covers and book trailers on a dare from her two sons.

Elizabeth loves the outdoors. In the summertime, you can find her in her secret garden with her laptop, swinging in her hammock working on her next book. Elizabeth is a born storyteller and passionate about sharing her works with her readers.

Please be sure to visit her website at **Elizabethrosenovels.com** to read excerpts from any of her novels and get sneak peeks at covers of upcoming books. You can follow her on **Twitter, Facebook, Goodreads** or **BookBub.** Be sure to sign up for her **newsletter** so you don't miss out on new releases or upcoming events.

ALSO BY ELIZABETH ROSE

Medieval

Legendary Bastards of the Crown Series

Seasons of Fortitude Series

Secrets of the Heart Series

Legacy of the Blade Series

Daughters of the Dagger Series

MadMan MacKeefe Series

Barons of the Cinque Ports Series

Second in Command Series

Medieval/Paranormal

Elemental Series

Greek Myth Fantasy Series

Tangled Tales Series

Contemporary

Tarnished Saints Series

Western

Cowboys of the Old West Series

Please visit http://elizabethrosenovels.com

Made in the USA
Monee, IL
10 August 2021

75338068R00135